Fred Beauford, Book Reviews

American Literary History

The Black American Long Struggle

American Presidents and Notables

Americana

The World

Foreword by Michael Moréau

A Neworld Review book, an imprint of

Morton Books, Inc

ISBN: 978-1929188-31-4

ISBN: 1-929188-31-5

Literary History

Literary Brooklyn: The Writers of Brooklyn and the Story of American City Life
by Evan Hughes

Reviewed by Fred Beauford

On the Waterfront

I have a confession to make that might just shock some old-time readers of this magazine, given my ongoing, shameless display of Bronx chauvinism, and my obvious distaste for and love of bashing Brooklyn every chance I get.

In the army, as a teenage wise guy from New York City, I strutted about like a young peacock, grabbing my crotch at every chance, and talked much trash and acted like the know-it-all I still am.

I told all the guys I was from Brooklyn, trying my best to talk out of the side of my mouth, as they looked on at me in slightly baffled amusement.

For some reason, Brooklyn just sounded more badass than being from the unsung Bronx, with only the white shoe Yankees to brag about.

There, it's finally off my chest, and I feel better already.

***

Brooklyn outclassed us rubes in the Bronx in terms of literary output as well, not satisfied with being the widely acknowledged tough guys of New York City. In fact, Evan Hughes' highly entertaining literary history lesson, *Literary Brooklyn: The Writers of Brooklyn and the Story of American City Life,* shows us that Brooklyn also gave Manhattan's famed Greenwich Village a run for its money as a haven for creative writers.

We touched on this once in the *Neworld Review,* in Jan Alexander's groundbreaking essay on Carson McCullers, and her stay at 7 Middagh Street in Brooklyn Heights, made famous in the book, *February House* by Sherill Tippins, which she shared with, among others, W.H. Auden, Klaus Mann and Gypsy Rose Lee.

Hughes gives us engaging portraits of off and on Brooklyn literary residents like Walt Whitman, Henry Miller, Hart Crane, Marianne Moore,

Thomas Wolfe, Richard Wright, the aforementioned in *February House*, Truman Capote, William Styron and Norman Mailer, among others.

His concise, well-researched biographic sketches of the writers in *Literary Brooklyn* are fully brought to life, and are alone well worth the price of the book.

***

Because this is also a book about the physical and economic development of Brooklyn, Hughes provides the proper context for why it became such a magnet for literary types.

When Walt Whitman, "the grandfather of literary Brooklyn," first arrived as a child of three, in 1823, "it was a place so different from the huge urban mass of today…that it is scarcely possible to hold it in the mind's eye," Hughes writes.

One interesting historical tidbit around this time jumped out at me from his book: "In 1800, before slaveholding was abolished in New York State, in 1827, about 60 percent of the white households within Brooklyn's current borders owned at least one slave, the highest proportion in the North," he writes.

In the first years of his 30s, Whitman was writing his self-published masterpiece, *Leaves of Grass*, which Hughes points out, "drew breath from the people of Brooklyn." A little over ten years later, at the eve of the Civil War, Brooklyn had grown from a quiet little village of five thousand during Whitman's childhood, to the nation's third largest city.

"Part of what spurred the growth," Hughes writes, "was Brooklyn's investment in an industrial waterfront that competed with Manhattan's. By the time that Henry Miller's family moved to Williamsburg in the early 1890s soon after his birth, this is what Manhattan had become, *Harper's* magazine had noted a few decades earlier: 'What was then a decent and orderly town of moderate size, has been converted into a huge semi-barbarous metropolis—one half as luxurious and artistic as Paris, the other half as savage as Cairo and Constantinople—not well-governed, but simply not governed at all'."

Hughes points out that "by the time Miller was born, Brooklyn had become something of a release valve, a place New Yorkers came in search of a haven, but also a place where trouble tended to follow them."

And come they did. In fact, so many Jews fled the crowded tenements of lower Manhattan that soon over 40 percent of Jews in New York were living in Brooklyn. By this time, Brooklyn was no longer a separate city, but had joined with the rest of New York, much to the dismay of many of its citizens.

Manhattan was becoming a polarized place of lavish townhouses and mansions for the well-off, and dismal tenements for almost everyone else, which eventually led to the building of the famous brownstones that Brooklyn is still famous for, as well as attached houses and roomy apartment buildings, all kept to a smaller scale than Manhattan or the Bronx.

People got to know each other in Brooklyn neighborhoods, which only added to the borough's charm and rapid growth.

But a seamier side of Brooklyn had also begun to emerge, especially around the docks where most of the creative writers ended up because of the cheap rent (I can still hear Marlon Brando overacting in *On the Waterfront:* "I could have been a contender, instead of a bum.").

Longshoremen and sailors from all over the world, the marginal, the sex-obsessed and lowlifes of all kinds, ages, shapes, and colors, all crowded the many bars and dives that dotted the landscape.

Unlike the sedate poet Marianne Moore, who lived quietly further inland, in Fort Green with her mother, novelists like Henry Miller and Thomas Wolfe relished the constant two-fisted challenge to self from the docks, and drew much from the dangerous, volatile world of the waterfront.

For gay poets like W. H, Auden and Hart Crane, who often came back to their dwellings battered and bruised, had the thrilling adventure of cruising Sands Street, with its many "sailor bars," seeking that perfect sailor—the one that would most capture their imaginations, and provide the muse they long sought.

***

In time, due to the earlier influx of Jews, as noted, Brooklyn, starting with the depression years of the '30s, started producing an amazing group of Jewish writers. For most of these writers, it wasn't a tough guy persona, or even writing the great American novel, filled with the hapless riffraff of Sands Street, they wanted most to write about.

What they wanted to project to the world was raw intelligence, the value of education, knowing things, and deep insights into the human condition. In other words, there was nothing wrong with being an intellectual.

Evan Hughes once again is highly impressive with his portraits of Daniel Fuchs, Bernard Malamud, and Alfred Kazin, among others.

***

Another American mass movement of people also took place, which would soon have a tremendous impact on Brooklyn: the great migration of millions of blacks fleeing the fascist South. Here is where Richard Wright takes center stage in *Literary Brooklyn.*

Richard Wright is more than just a footnote in American literary history. He was one of the first that held up the unblinking mirror to America, both black and white, that said, this is who you really are.

He wrote his two most famous books, *Native Son*, and *Black Boy* in Brooklyn.

***

Literary Brooklyn skillfully brings us up to present day Brooklyn, after taking the reader through the great collapse of the wartime economy, including another interesting historical tidbit: The Brooklyn Navy Yard produced more ships during World War Two than all of Japan!

We start to see rapid urban decline and despair, reflected best by Hubert Selby Jr.'s grim, in your face *Last Exit to Brooklyn,* and Arthur Miller's tale of economic defeat in *Death of a Salesman*, which had Brooklyn written all over it, but which struck a chord with all of Americans, most of whom were enduring some of the same change of events, often with the same dismal results that the confused, deeply disappointed Willy Loman faced.

***

In the end, Brooklyn was slowly brought back to life, first by the pioneering "brownstoners," who bought sturdy, but well-worn dwellings (a special nod should go to those many African American women who have helped maintain this historical housing), when no one with any good sense wanted to come anywhere near certain areas of Brooklyn. Then the artists started coming, led by people like filmmaker Spike Lee, and the Village Voice writer Nelson George.

Suddenly, Brooklyn was cool again.

Again, like in years past, it offered the affordable rent that one could not find in Manhattan, as even the once trashy East Village was now overrun with big pocketed, Wall Street types.

Hughes gives us a passing look at present day Brooklyn creative writers including Jhumpa Lahiri, Colson Whitehead, Jennifer Egan, Rick Moody, Jonathan Safran Foer, Susan Choi, Nathan Englander, Nicole Krauss, Darin Strauss, Kurt Andersen, Arthur Phillips, Julie Orringer, Rivka Galchen, Keith Gessen, Hannah Tinti, Tim McLoughlin and Jonathan Ames.

***

Literary Brooklyn: The Writers of Brooklyn and the Story of American City Life is a wonderful literary history lesson, well told, and I was sad that it had to end. I once again thank my friends at Henry Holt for sending me yet another compelling book to review, and thank author Evan Hughes for writing it; and if he would ever like to write for the *Neworld Review,* he is more than welcome.

It's books like *Literary Brooklyn* that cause you to not only walk the streets of Brooklyn, but also Manhattan, my beloved Bronx, Queens, and even lowly Staten Island, all of which have played huge roles in America's literary history—and hear countless stories, some beyond awful, some beyond wonderful, some beyond belief—and makes one feel proud to have grown up in New York, and to have reached one of the highest honors this great city bestows, that of a literary editor and publisher.

Rebel Souls: Walt Whitman and America's First Bohemians

By Justin Martin

Da Capo Press

Reviewed by Fred Beauford

Seeking A Caliphate

The one great thing about living in this country, because of its newness,
and vast space, is that my follow countrymen (and women) can still
organize societies based on religion, race and income. Rich people, middle
class folks, Jews, Amish, blacks, whites and others, can live most of their
lives in America and never interact with anyone other than their group, and
be happily left alone.

There is one group, however, where this is not the case: creative artists,
once even labeled Bohemians. Wherever they have tried to build a
community, be it in North Beach, San Francisco; Venice Beach in Los

Angeles; or Greenwich Village and SoHo in Manhattan, they were soon overrun by their arch enemy, the mighty money grubbers who follows them everywhere they go, grimly determined to find out what their secrets are, and how could they get some of it for themselves.

Now, politicians all across the country have gotten in the act, hoping to prop up rundown city centers. They are courting artists to come and save them. In Detroit, for example, they even have a plan where they will sell a house to an artist for one dollar if they promise to stay in it for four years.

But just whom are these politicians trying to fool anyway? They don't really want these unkempt artists; and by now, the artists know it. They know that they are just being used as bait, because anyone in the know, knows that the evil moneygrubbers will quickly descend on them, despite their being the blazing wits and cutups that they are—like a pack of hungry hyenas; and, they bring with them countless millions in new revenue.

***

Rebel Souls offers us a highly informative look at the very first attempt here in America for novelists, poets, actors, dancers, visual artists and journalists, to together and try to create a society. They called themselves Bohemians.

Martin first gives us a detailed history of the term "Bohemian." It dates, he writes, "to roughly 1830. Its coinage is rooted in a misperception, namely, that the Romani people (Gypsies) who were wandering into France during the nineteenth century were natives of Bohemia, then a central European Kingdom.

"Well-to-do, establishment Parisians—especially those of a conservative political bent—applied it to the Romani, but also to anyone who looked eccentric: Flamboyantly dressed artists, scruffy students, women of suspect moral standing…Parisian artists and other free-living types seized on *Bohemian*, appropriated it, made it their own. The word made it possible to contrast two opposing forces in society. You had your bourgeois—cautious, smug, and prosperous. And you had their opposite: Bohemians. In France, *Bohemian* quickly became tightly packed with cultural coding. Utter but that single word, and a vivid image unfolded."

Enter a newspaperman and political activist from New England named Henry Clapp Jr. In August 1849, Clapp went to Paris to attend a three-day world peace congress, where he found a city that had just experienced a revolution the year before he arrived, and "the boulevards of Paris still thrummed with idealism, slogans and grand artistic schemes. The city's cafes played host to a thriving scene, known as Bohemianism."

Captivated by what he saw, Clapp decided to stay awhile. He stayed for over four years.

After the experience of Paris, and the vibrant artistic atmosphere—made even more so by the instant sensation on November 22, 1849 of the play *La Vie de Boheme,* which Puccini later adapted in 1896 for his classic opera, *La Boheme*—there was no way that Clapp could return to New England.

Instead, he moved to New York City, determined to bring to America the Bohemia he had experience in Paris.

"In 1856 he happened upon a promising venue for this experience: Pfaff's Restaurant and Lager Bier Saloon," says Martin.

Pfaff's was situated beneath the fashionable Coleman House at the corner of Broadway and Bleecker Street (I must have walked by this spot thousands of times, not knowing the history that was right under my feet)

Writes Martin: "Clapp had found his Cafe Momus. He'd discovered a place with the right permissive air, a Manhattan equivalent to the Paris haunt of Henry Murger (co-author of *La Vie de Boheme*) and friends. Now, it was just a matter of assembling a coterie of Bohemians."

Bringing together such a group, which ultimately included Walt Whitman, and, what was unheard of, women, was skillfully accomplished by Clapp. As the news of this offbeat group of artists, and now famous bar, spread across the country, Clapp became known as "The King of Bohemia"; and although he died not having a hint of what was to come, what he started began a slow but sure shift of the literary world from Boston and New England to New York City.

Like Paris at the time Clapp spent there, America was also entering into a dark, dangerous time in its history, as the question of slavery could no longer be ignored.

Martin points out, "The fact that Clapp was able to launch an American Bohemia during the 1950s is not mere happenstance. Conditions were ripe. Just as revolutionary rumblings had caused Paris's Left Bank scene to blossom in the 1840s, America was going through paroxysm of it own in the decade that came to known as the Fiery Fifties."

Despite all of this background noise, or maybe because of it, artists continued to be artists, and now some of them had found a home of their own thanks to Pfaff's, and the work of the historically unsung Henry Clapp Jr.

Martin does an excellent job in *Rebel Souls*, of drawing insightful portraits of some of the main characters like Whitman, which is the heart of his book.

The war years saw the slow breakup of Clapp's collection of remarkably talented artists that sat at the long table especially set aside in a vaulted room at Pfaff's. For example, Walt Whitman left for Washington, where he nursed wounded soldiers. It was also there where he met Peter Doyle, who became the love of his life.

And, by now, Bohemianism had spread west and found a home in San Francisco (see my review *The Bohemians: Mark Twain and the San Francisco Writers Who Reinvented American Literature,* By Ben Tarnoff, issue No.49).

In 1865, with the war only two months over, Clapp, hoping to reconstitute his status as "The King of Bohemia," restarted his publication, *Saturday Press,* which had done wonders to gain recognition for what he brought to America from Paris. He managed a few publishing coups, including publishing Mark Twain's *Jim Smiley and his Jumping Frog,* which caused a sensation.

"Twain's reputation," writes Martin, "was strictly regional. But after appearing, first in the *Saturday Press*, the story was reproduced across the United States...Clapp, champion of Whitman, also gave Twain his first big national break."

But Clapp's publication soon floundered. Its last issue was June 2, 1866. Clapp died penniless on April 10, 1875. He was sixty years old. As Martin notes, he was born a Puritan, and died a Bohemian.

The Bohemians: Mark Twain and the San Francisco Writers Who Reinvented American Literature

By Ben Tarnoff

Reviewed by Fred Beauford

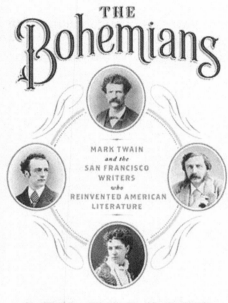

The Freedom of Isolation

For me, the major lesson I learned once again from *The Bohemians*—

and a lesson I have harped on many times in my writings in these pages—

is that the literature of the New World is a dynamic, ever growing narrative.

In addition, it is composed of multiple streams of thought pushed

forward by independent-minded thinkers.

One key to these thinkers being able to think for themselves was to get as far away as they could from all the clerics and nabobs that insisted that they think in a certain way; and mid-19th century San Francisco, the first real unban center on the Pacific coast, offered such a place.

San Francisco rose up because the San Francisco Bay offered one of the world's greatest natural ports for shipping,

In addition, it also offered a gateway to Asia.

Still, in 1848, the same year that the Treaty of Guadalupe ended the Mexican-American War and gave California to the United States, San Francisco was hardly much of an urban center, with a little over 40,000 residents, overwhelmingly men.

All of this changed almost at the blink of an eye. Writes Tarnoff," In 1848, the discovery of gold in California (which must have greatly pissed off the Mexicans to have lost such a treasure) had triggered a swift influx of people from all corners of the world. As the gateway to the gold rush, San Francisco went from a drowsy backwater to a booming global seaport. Mostly the newcomers were young men.... They lived among the cultures of five continents...Cantonese stir-fry competing with German wurst,

Chilean whores with Australians. On the far margin of the continent, they created a complex urban society virtually overnight."

The Bohemians profiles in depth, and interesting, telling details, four writers, all in their twenties, that formed the core group of writers Tarnoff labels The Bohemians: Samuel Clemens (Mark Twain) Bret Harte, Charles Warren Stoddard and Ina Coolbrith.

The most well known, Mark Twain, fearing being caught up the Civil War, arrived by stagecoach in San Francisco in 1863 after several years in Nevada. Bret Harte, who was already a fairly well-known poet and short story writer when Twain arrived, first stepped foot in Oakland in 1854 as a seventeen-year-old from New York; the gay poet Stoddard, also a New Yorker, arrived in 1855, at age eleven.

The most interesting of the four for this reader, and the only woman, was Ina Coolbrith. And quite a story the melancholy poet had to tell. Her father died five months after she was born in 1841. Her uncle was none other than Joseph Smith, the Mormon prophet. When Ina was three, Smith died in an Illinois jail, murdered by a mob.

In 1851 her stepfather led her family West, where at the foot of the Sierra Nevada, the family met Jim Beckwourth, a freed slave turned Crow chieftain. He had recently discovered a path through the Sierras—the famous Beckwourth Pass.

Writes Tarnoff, "She remembers him as 'one of the most beautiful creatures that ever lived.'" who said to her and her sisters after he had led them in sight of the other side, "Here is California, little girls, here is your kingdom."

The family settled in Los Angeles, where she found local fame as a poet. But grief continued to follow her, including giving birth to a child that died, and a deranged and jealous husband who tried to kill her and her mother, saved only after her stepfather shot him in the hand as he was attacking them.

Notes Tarnoff, "She loved Lord Byron, and her ordeal made her more Byronic: an outcast with a secret past."

"Only twenty, and my world turned to dusk," she wrote.

Like Byron, she went into exile, embarking to San Francisco in 1862.

A year later, when Mark Twain rode into town on his stagecoach from Virginia City, Nevada, this was not the San Francisco of the Gold Rush. Writes Tarnoff, "By the time Twain got there, San Francisco still roared. It was densely urban, yet unmistakably western; isolated yet cosmopolitan; crude yet cultured…. Even as the gold rush waned, and the miners' shanties became banks and restaurants and boutiques, the city didn't slow to a more settle rhythm, Rather, it financed the opening of new frontiers—in Nevada, Idaho, and elsewhere—and leaped from one bonanza to the next."

In other words, by the 1860s, San Francisco reigned over a flourishing economic empire.

What was more important for Twain, Harte, Stoddard and Coolbrith was that San Francisco also supported a thriving publishing culture.

"California was always crawling with scribblers," Tarnoff points out.

Harte, as the most recognized literary light in the city, led the way. As a columnist for the leading literary weekly on the Pacific coast, the *Golden Era,* he began calling himself The Bohemian. By 1863, all four were writing for the *Golden Era.*

"Under the banner of Bohemia, these four writers competed, collaborated, traded counsel and criticism. Some remained friends their whole lives. Others became bitter enemies. What connected them was their contempt for custom and their restlessness with received wisdom. They belonged to Bohemia because they didn't belong anywhere else," Tarnoff writes.

As we well know, only Mark Twain received worldwide recognition and had a profound impact on American literature. Harte and Stoddard had limited success outside of San Francisco, with Harte flashing boldly on the larger national literary stage for a few minutes, but quickly fading. No such national recognition happened to the haunted Coolbrith. She became a librarian in Oakland, but did find recognition late in life, as she became the first California poet laureate.

As she accepted her reward in San Francisco at the age of seventy-four, in 1915, she quietly said to the crowded auditorium:

"I feel that the honor extended me today is meant not so much because of any special merit of my own, as in memory of that wonderful group of early California writers with which it was my fortune to be affiliated, and of which I am the sole survivor."

Nothing I could write could better sum up this book. *The Bohemians* is an excellent American literary history lesson, well worth spending some time with.

The City of Light and the Making of American Writers

An essay by Fred Beauford

Hemingway

For reasons I cannot fully understand, for the last few years I have

become obsessed with reading biographies of 20th Century American

writers—madly almost, until book after book finally led me to those writers

who came to the conclusion that exile from America was the only way they

could ever fully realize their talents as creative writers in a uncharted post

war world, first with Ernest Hemingway's Lost Generation and their long,

slow journey by sea to the fable City of Light.

Hemingway's shell-shocked generation was still walking in the bloody footsteps of the most horrendous shedding of human blood by other humans in recorded history—what we call World War I.

It was also clear that The Lost Generation was seeking small, fun-filled caves with like-minded souls, to slowly lick their wounds and seek something meaningful other than material things and more warfare.

American writers first discovered Paris as *the* place to be for artists because of a newspaperman and political activist from New England named Henry Clapp Jr. In August 1849, Clapp went to Paris to attend a three-day world peace congress, where he found a city that had just experienced a revolution the year before he arrived, and "the boulevards of Paris still thrummed with idealism, slogans and grand artistic schemes. The city's cafes played host to a thriving scene, known as Bohemianism," writes Justin Martin in *Rebel Souls: Walt Whitman and America's First Bohemians*

After the experience of Paris, and the vibrant artistic atmosphere—made even more so by the instant sensation on November 22, 1849 of the play *La Vie de Boheme,* which Puccini later adapted in 1896 for his classic opera, *La Boheme*—there was no way that Clapp could return to New England. Instead, he moved to New York City, determined to bring to

America the Bohemia he had experience in Paris. And bring it he did, and he single-handedly started the mystique of The City of Light in America.

***

It was Gertrude Stein—Paris's abiding spirit and prominent literary hostess—who coined the phrase "The Lost Generation" in conversation with Ernest Hemingway.

"You are all a lost generation," she said to him.

These "lost" American writers that often cross path with Stein and Hemingway included Hart Crane, Ezra Pound and F. Scott Fitzgerald and his wife, the notorious Zelda Fitzgerald of legend.

Notwithstanding the highly entertaining drunken antics of the Fitzgerald's, my personal favorites among this crowd of lost souls from America, have always been Sara Murphy, and her husband, the sometimes painter Gerald Murphy.

Although marginally literary, the two were both being exceptionally good looking; and they were also very rich, fashionable, loved writers, and were well known for the famous line "living well is the best revenge."

During this period the American exile writers encountered not only the Murphys, but interacted with "any number of intersecting artistic cliques including Modernists and Cubists, Dadaists and Futurists, Expressionists and Surrealists. These were the years of Picasso and Modigliani, Braque and Duchamp, Stravinsky and Satie, Diaghilev and Cocteau. Radical developments in the visual and performing arts were mirrored in the Continental literature of the time, from the surrealist shock tactics of André Bréton and Guillaume Apollinaire, to the textual experimentation of Joyce and Beckett. It was into this vibrant, inspiring foment of idea and innovation that the self-imposed exiles of America's 'Lost Generation' flung themselves."

(Editor's note: this highly dramatic quote is from a book entitled *The Lost Generation*, but as I tried to find the exact book it was taken from, and posted online, I found over 500 titles of the same name. Obviously, The Lost Generation has had its fair share of admirers).

***

And, after another horrifying world war in as little as twenty years later, we find American writers once again trying to make sense of a world that seems to go mad every twenty years, almost on cue.

During most of the late '40s and early '50s, American intellectuals and artists, as shell-shocked as the Lost Generation, having witnessed slaughter beyond belief, ended up once again in the same place as *The Lost Generation: the Fabled City of Light*, Paris.

Now we have yet another great wave of American artists infatuated with Paris. Even black American writers like Richard Wright, James Baldwin, the often overlooked Chester Himes, the then-dancer, poet/memoirist Maya Angelou, all fled to Paris, where they encountered Simone de Beauvoir, Edith Piaf, Jean Paul Sartre, a much older Pablo Picasso, Albert Camus, and countless white American writers like James Jones, Norman Mailer, Christopher Isherwood, Saul Bellow, Philip Roth and Truman Capote, all doing the "Paris bohemian thing," as Baldwin might say.

And as much as these brilliant writers felt that they had to flee an uptight, militaristic, anti-gay, anti-interracial coupling, racist America, most soon realized that they were Americans after all, that there was indeed something called an American.

When they looked at each closely, they saw a part of themselves, especially when they discovered how marginalized the Arabs were in France. Black and white, gay or not, well off, or barely getting by, they immediately recognized what that was all about. They had grown up with these kinds of characters, and came to the City of Light in the first place, to get away from them. But there they now were.

And, like the Lost Generation before them, these writers also had an even stronger pull back to America. France was still suffering from the last war, and was trying to hold on to what was left of its once mighty colonial power, especially Algeria.

America was never a real colonial player, like Britain and France, and after both world wars, it quickly went back to what it did best: make a lot of people rich. This country was still the most dynamic country on earth, and there were grants, awards, and magazines to write for; book companies were pining away for their services. And there was the new thing called television, which could give them more fame than they ever hoped for.

And once again, what really made America exciting for these creative writers, like those ex-pats before then, was this was where the action was, where clouds of turmoil were slowly gathering, where it looked as if old wounds could at last be addressed.

What else could such a writer want? This was the New World.

Richard Wright and Chester Himes, with Himes finally settling in Franco's Spain, refused to leave Europe. Henry Miller stayed longer then most, and James Baldwin never fully gave up on France, and spent most of his adult life going back and forth between the two counties, with many stops in Istanbul. He died at the age of 63, December 1, 1987 at Saint-Paul de Vence in the south of France.

Those that left for good did not give up bohemia, however, when they decided to return home, and stayed true to their bohemian roots, started by Henry Clapp, and soon settled in North Beach in San Francisco, and Greenwich Village in New York City, which had become mother's milk for creative writers and essayists, despite the heady hedonism of wine, women (and hot young boys) and American jazz, of Paris.

"Yes, I am an American," most ultimately said, including a deeply conflicted, wavering Baldwin, who despite his saying he just wanted to be left alone to pursue his art became the spokesman and conscience of the Civil Rights Generation in America, and like the others, sailed back home more than eager to join in the debate that was now unfolding in his country.

Wear and Tear: The Threads of My Life

A memoir by Tracy Tynan

Reviewed by Fred Beauford

Beware of Being Born to Artists

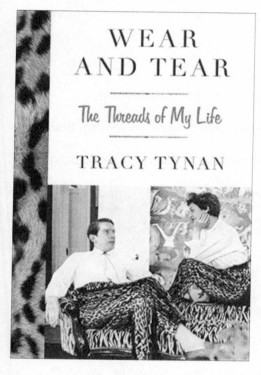

"Tracy Tynan uses the universal medium of clothing to tell the highly specific story of her bohemian British upbringing, and she does so with wit, candor, and yes—style."

Lena Dunham

Lena Dunham's cover blurb summarizes this book quite nicely. For me, however, the clothing aspect of *Wear and Tear* takes a decidedly back seat to the often-horrific home environment that the author had to grow up in, being the only child of renowned theater critic Kenneth Tynan and novelist Elaine Dundy.

One was a chain-smoking drama queen, the other a bi-poplar unpredictable mess. Both were chronic alcoholics, with her mother also becoming a pill-popping drug addict. But both could be extremely charming, well dressed, and social, and they loved parties and witty, famous people— people they collected the same way some people collect stamps, or first editions of novels.

Tynan writes, "I lived in a flat with my often irritable, unpredictable mother and my nervous, chain-smoking father, who was forever struggling to meet writing deadlines. We never ate dinner, or any meal together. My mother did not cook. Very occasionally we ate together at restaurants, but these were usually large social occasions where I just happened to be included. Most of the time I ate alone or with the *au pair*, who probably would've preferred to be out with friends her own age."

After I read a few more chapters, not knowing what else to expect from this book, I kept thinking Scottie, Scottie. And soon, there it was on page 42:

"My parents frequently separated. My mother even got an apartment of her own for a while. I always stayed with my father and an *au pair* at the Mount Street flat. During one of the separations, my father went to Malaga for the bullfighting festival. A few days after he left, my mother followed, checking into the same hotel, the Miramar, and immediately taking up with a handsome Scottish laird, Peter Combe. I can only attribute her choices to the fact that both of my parents seemed to revel in humiliation in front of each other and in public, trying their best to be the Scott and Zelda Fitzgerald of the '50s. Epic fights took place, which exhausted their friends. Once my father broke my mother's nose...."

Poor, Frances Scott "Scottie" Fitzgerald, the only daughter and child of F. Scott and Zelda, had to endure much of the same things that Tracy Tynan endured, including seeing her mother end up in a mental hospital, as had Scottie's.

What I found most interesting, is that growing up with all the craziness, the non-stop celebrity parties that her parents were always attending or throwing in London, and in New York City two years, when Kenneth Tynan was theater critic for *The New Yorker,* Tracy lived a very grounded life, although she once flirted with cocaine and pot, and once considered herself a hippie.

It was clearly her love of interesting clothing that kept her centered. In the very first chapter she makes this crystal clear: "I think I was destined to be obsessed with clothing, genetically speaking. My middle name is Peacock. My father, Kenneth Peacock Tynan, was a writer and theater critic, but before he had ever published a single sentence, he was known for his unique style of dress....The writer Paul Johnson, in his book, *Modern Times*, described my father as a 'tall, beautiful, epicene youth, with pale yellow locks, Beardsley cheekbones, fashionable stammer, plum-colored suit, lavender tie and ruby signet ring'."

Tracy also pointed out that her mother "was no slouch in the clothing department, either."

This love of walking the streets of London, and later New York City and Los Angeles, looking for something different, clever, and exciting to wear, led Tracy into a career in film as a costume designer. Her credits include *The Big Easy, Blind Date. Great Balls of Fire* (which her husband, Jim McBride, directed), and *Tuesdays with Morrie.*

This is a most interesting book.

Mario Puzo: An American Writer's Quest

By M. J. Moore

Heliotrope Books | 2019

Reviewed by Fred Beauford

A Quest Indeed!

There was one missing aspect of Moore's exceptional book detailing

the ups and downs of author Mario Puzo in his quest to be recognized as a gifted writer of refined, literary novels—a quest that he never fully was able to achieve.

The world of literary fiction books in the '50s and '60s was centered in Manhattan and it was mainly a world of WASPS, Jews and a few other Northern Europeans. They were the writers, editors, agents, and critics of books, magazines and newspapers. There were also a few late-night NYC local television shows that featured authors. (One famous night I stayed up late to watch *enfant terrible* Truman Capote when he was asked what he thought of Jack Kerouac's *On The Road*? "That was not writing; that was typing" he said in that famous voice of his in one of the greatest literary put-downs in American history! I laughed my teenage ass off.)

However, there were few Italians to speak of. As a result, look at this bird's-eye view of some of the important books of the '50s, to see what I mean: Patricia Highsmith, *Strangers on a Train* (1950), C. S. Lewis, *The Lion, the Witch, and the Wardrobe* (1950), James Jones, *From Here to Eternity*, Josephine Tey, *The Daughter of Time* (1951), Ernest Hemingway, *The Old Man and the Sea* (1952), Patricia Highsmith, *The Price of Salt* (1952), Bernard Malamud, *The Natural* (1952), Flannery O'Connor, *Wise Blood* (1952), Barbara Pym, *Excellent Women* (1952), John Steinbeck, *East of Eden* (1952), Kurt Vonnegut, *Piano Player* (1952), E. B. White,

Charlotte's Web (1952), Ralph Ellison, *Invisible Man*, 1953, Raymond Chandler, *The Long Goodbye* (1953), James Baldwin, *Go Tell it on the Mountain* (1953), Gwendolyn Brooks, *Maud Martha* (1953), William S. Burroughs, *Junky* (1953), J. D. Salinger, *Nine Stories* (1953), William Golding, *Lord of the Flies* (1954), Wallace Stevens, *Collected Poems* (1954), Richard Matheson, *I Am Legend* (1954), Patricia Highsmith, The *Talented Mr. Ripley* (1955), J. P. Donleavy, *The Ginger Man* (1955), Graham Greene, *The Quiet American* (1955), Flannery O'Connor, *A Good Man is Hard to Find and Other Stories* (1955), John Ashbery, Some Trees (1956), Gerald Durrell, *My Family and Other Animals* (1956), Dodie Smith, *The Hundred and One Dalmatians* (1956), James Baldwin, *Giovanni's Room* (1956), Allen Ginsberg, *Howl and Other Poems* (1956), John Cheever, *The Wapshot Chronicle* (1957), Roland Barthes, *Mythologies* (1957), Bernard Malamud, *The Assistant* (1957), Nevil Shute, *On the Beach* (1957), Truman Capote, *Breakfast at Tiffany's* (1958), Graham Greene, *Our Man in Havana* (1958), Jack Kerouac, *The Dharma Bums* (1958), T. H. White, *The Once and Future King* (1958), Robert Bloch, *Psycho* (1959), Philip Roth, *Goodbye, Columbus* (1959), William S. Burroughs, *Naked Lunch* (1959), Shirley Jackson, *The Haunting of Hill House* (1959), John Knowles, *A Separate Peace* (1959).

This was quite an array of exceptional literary talent. Just looking at these titles, you can see that this was an incredible output never seen in America before, and this was just a snapshot of an even larger output. Also, note that black Americans writers' names were also called, although there were almost no blacks working in the literary world as editors or publishers or agents during this period. What they had going for them, besides talent, was the enormous roar of *Brown v. Board of Education* and the start of the Civil Rights Movement in the South.

However, in the literary world of New York City in the '50s and '60s, where were the Italian Americans, whose names were rarely called in one of the most exciting literary times in American history?

Here is how Moore fully capsulized the '50s and early '60s: "To be an aspiring writer in those years was to have at least some sense of being at the red-hot center of a vibrant, important, national culture. Regardless of whatever had accompanied anyone's quest to become a published author, it was clear in season after season that strong talents could be remembered, and superlatives works were able to make it through the pipeline of the publishing industry."

Puzo's first attempt to join this crowd was his first novel *The Dark Arena*. He was turned down by several publishers but was finally picked up by Random House. Writes Moore, "Random House, the largest and at that time the most prestigious American publisher, brought *The Dark Arena* on January 20, 1954. They paid a tiny sum in the form of an advance. By this time Mario was again working full-time at a civil service job."

I should point out that Puzo was married and had three young children to feed at this time.

The novel went nowhere. Writes Moore, "Critiques of *The Dark Arena* ranged from laudatory and welcoming to dismissive and downright insulting. The novel provoked serious reactions, one way or the other."

It wasn't until 1964 was his second novel, *The Fortunate Pilgrim* was put into production. It seemed that Mario Puzo was on his way to fame and fortune when the book was finally published.

"When published in January 1965, the novel received the praise all writers long for," writes Moore.

The New York Times, *The Saturday Review of Literature* and, many other magazines and newspapers heaped honors on him. One critic even compared him to Hemingway. And, to top it off, a noted Hollywood producer, John Foreman, took him to lunch.

"John Foreman was dynamic," Mario recalled. "For three hours he talked about my book, how he loved it. How he was determined to do a movie. He quoted all the best parts. As he left, he said he would call my agent the next day and arrange the financial details of the contract. Nobody ever heard from him again."

In the end, *The Fortunate Pilgrim*, made even less money than his first novel. His first novel from 1955 netted him $3,500 and the second one in 1965 netted him $3,000. Writes Puzo to a friend, "I was going downhill fast. Yet the book (*The Fortunate Pilgrim*) received some extraordinarily fine reviews. *The New York Times* called it 'A small classic.' I immodestly think of it as art."

For the next few years, Puzo wrote pulp fiction for men's magazines that were several steps down from *Playboy*. He also now had five off-spring to support. He soon became a master of this kind of fiction and was able to keep his head above water and feed his growing family. But still he pined for recognition as an important writer.

Puzo tried hard to find another publisher for a novel he had in mind, with no takers. Yet a publisher set off a chain reaction by remarking that "If *Fortunate Pilgrim* had only had a little more of the Mafia stuff in it the book would have made money."

The passage of time had not dimmed America's perennial fascination with gangster tales. What we had in the '50s was televised congressional hearings about organized crime, and in the early '60s we heard the testimony of Joseph Valachi, a lifelong criminal. Writes Moore, he had "deep roots in the Sicilian-based East-Coast mob network who explained in his testimony what Cosa Nostra was all about." The American public also had the hit television show *The Untouchables* to watch weekly.

It didn't take long for Puzo to catch on. All those years writing pulp fiction to feed his family, as well as writing a literary masterpiece like the *Fortunate Pilgrim* you can almost see the light bulb going off in his head: why not combine both into one novel?

The results were *The Godfather*, which became the bestselling book of all time worldwide, next to the Bible, and two of the greatest movies ever made in Hollywood. The middle-aged, overweight father of five, with the same wife until her death, finally made quite a name for himself. M. J. Moore also has made quite a name for himself by writing this excellent book.

Book Cover Designs

Edited by Matthew Goodman

Reviewed by Fred Beauford

When I received an email from Schiffer Publishing, a book publishing company I was not familiar with, I knew immediately that the book they were pitching to me, *Book Cover Designs*, was one I had to personally review.

I have done much with book covers at *Neworld Review,* as you well know. I learned years ago, as a print magazine editor-in-chief, that print and visual art compliment each other in so many ways.

But now what? What about this brand-new online world? This is not the large, wonderful space you have with an 8 1/2-by-11 format, or a "double truck," as the case may be.

So, how do you marry the best of both worlds?

One day, as I was sitting in my office in New York City (the barstool at The Garage in the Village), I was thinking about all the wonderful books that had started pouring into *Neworld Review*, my first venture into this new world.

It hit me: those great looking book covers would make better art than author's photos. Most writers are not noted for their good looks, anyway.

It was clearly an impolite thought on my part about my good, faithful friends, the writers; but nevertheless, I immediately took them off of the home page, and started using the book covers as art; and here we are, almost ten years later, and those great covers certainly did help to put us on the map.

In fact, I spotted at least four of them in Goodman's book that I have used for art. It was also good to see the faces of the artists that produced those covers.

Matthew Goodman does a great job in his selections, as he looked at the work of countless dozens of book cover designers, both individuals and design companies. In the end, out of this, he selected 51. He also had all of his selections to write a brief reason for their many successes in their field.

Most of Goodman's selections in *Book Cover Designs* worked very well as both art and as a selling tool. Because, in the end, and I don't have to tell you this, book readers, if the buyers don't know in a few seconds just what this book could be about, the design means nothing, a total failure, no matter how great the art is.

One of the major jobs of the editor-in-chief, as I well know, is to keep a sharp eye on the art directors, especially if they are brilliant, and don't let them get carried away. In Goodman's book, a few of his subjects did just that, and made me go, "Now what is this all about?"

But they were few.

It is also interesting to note just how evenly this most compelling, yet quiet branch of art directing is spilt so evenly between male and female artists. Maybe this just Goodman being politically correct, or maybe this is just the case. Let's hope so.

This book would make a nice present on any occasion for that bookworm friend or relative. Race, color or creed, we all are grateful that we all have at least one of them. This bookworm certainly found *Book Cover Designs* quite interesting.

Jeff Herman's Guide to Book Publisher, Editors and Literary Agents

By Jeff Herman

Reviewed by Fred Beauford

More Meat Than I Thought

I have often turned to Jeff Herman's continuously updated guide to book

publishers, editors and literary agents. When I first started writing, years

ago, I turned to it in seeking an agent. His book lists hundreds of agents,

most of who, as expected, work in New York City.

When I started *Neworld Review* in 2007, Herman's book was really a

godsend, because I was able to used it to contact publishers, editors and

publicity departments at "a numerically tiny oligarchy of multinational,

trillion-dollar conglomerates," independent presses and university presses.

This provided me with a ready stream of book and publishing information that allowed me to stay up to date with the latest trends in the publishing industry.

What was also invaluable was Herman's advice to new writers about how to avoid some of the scams that permeate the industry, as predators exploit would-be authors, authors that would do almost anything to get published.

"Bogus agents make money in countless ways," he writes, "other than by doing what real agents do. Bogus agents tend not to ever sell works to traditional publishers and don't operate on the basis of earning commissions. Instead, they may offer amazing promises and an itemized menu of non-agent services, like simply reading your works for a fee… If someone says she will be your agent and if you pay her money, then she isn't a bona fide agent."

But the best point he made about the current state of the publishing industry reliance on agents as the gatekeepers was in his introduction: "In the beginning, my primary motive for doing this book was to give writers valuable information that was cloaked from them by habit, if not volition. It seemed that the screening process was unduly influenced by factors entirely separate from merit. Those who were fortunate enough to be from certain communities, to have attended certain schools, or to have the right connections were more likely to get published. If access to the process wasn't fairly distributed, it followed that the opportunities were rigged. Clearly, cultural constraints are harmful for society, whether imposed by a government or by inbred subcultures."

Enough said. Make of Jeff Herman's comments what you will, but I think he is on to something. *Guide to Book Publishers, Editors and Literary Agents* is highly recommended for would-be authors.

The Black American Struggle

Booker T. Washington Rediscovered
Edited by Michael Scott Bieze and Marybeth Gasman
Reviewed by Fred Beauford

"Cast down your bucket where you are." Booker T. Washington, 1895, in a speech before the Cotton States and International Exposition in Atlanta.

Once, when I was an undergraduate at New York University, I participated in a public debate. The question on the floor: Resolved, who was right, Booker T. Washington or Dr. W.E.B. Du Bois in regard to which direction Negroes should go?

Since I organized the debate, I assigned myself the role of Booker T. Washington, the second-ever nationally known black leader in America, following in the giant footsteps of Frederick Douglass, who has been called a founding father of African American education in the United States because he founded the famed Tuskegee Normal and Industrial Institute in 1891.

***

To this day, I am convinced that I could have won that debate if my opponent hadn't gone Baptist minister, and stomped all over me.

He quickly took over, and soon had the crowd in an uproar. My cool, impeccable logic meant little here.

Still, for most of my adult life, Booker T. Washington's main message has stayed with me: blacks needed to keep producing things, like they were once forced to do in slavery; and now make it work for them. I chose to take the role of Washington in that debate because I had felt that Booker T.

and I had reached the same conclusion: it was for very real reasons that black slaves were the most valuable people in the new world.

***

Booker T. Washington Rediscovered is a very interesting way to present both the ideas and the man behind them: a mixed-race ex-slave, who rose to become one of the most important figures in American life, and his fame became worldwide.

His book *Up from Slavery*, first published in 1901, has never gone out of print.

***

"In 1895," writes the online site historymatters.gmu.edu, "Booker T. Washington gave what later came to be known as the Atlanta Compromise speech before the Cotton States and International Exposition in Atlanta. His address was one of the most important and influential speeches in American history, guiding African-American resistance to white discrimination and establishing Washington as one of the leading black spokesmen in America. Washington's speech stressed accommodation rather than resistance to the racist order under which Southern African

Americans lived. In 1903, Washington recorded this portion of his famous speech, the only surviving recording of his voice."

Washington's many detractors, especially Dr. Du Bois, often cite this speech as proof that he had become the dreaded Uncle Tom, the turncoat, the sellout, the person all African Americans have been taught, for good reasons, for generations, to hate and despise, even more than the Northern European settlers.

***

We have none of this in *Booker T. Washington Rediscovered*. We meet Booker T. Washington through the many magazine articles he wrote, all in their original printed form, typos and all; and the many speeches he gave.

"Booker T. Washington," the editors write, "was once one of the Progressive Age's most popular speakers on both sides of the color line. His public speaking gift first received acclaim when a *New York Times* reporter mentioned the young Washington's skill in an article, after hearing Washington speak at his 1875 Hampton Institute graduation. Debating and public speaking became his passion."

As I read this, I once more marveled at the role great public speaking has played in human history. To repeat myself, the speech, it seems, has always been more compelling than either the pen, or the sword.

***

I would recommend this book to those who may have heard of the famed "Wizard of Tuskegee," but know little of what he stood for. With *Booker T. Washington Rediscovered*, we hear directly from him, with no historians, or political types with an axe to grind, or even being celebratory, weighing in.

Booker T. Washington was once one of the most famous persons in the world. The school he founded still educates scores of black people, both men and women. And it has served a great need, welcoming everyone from newly freed slaves, to the famous Tuskegee Airmen of World War Two.

Singer/songwriter Lionel Richie grew up on the campus of Tuskegee; his grandfather's house was right across the street from the home of the president of the college. It was there, later as a student, that he helped form The Commodores, who went on to have many national hit records.

Richie became a single act as a singer/songwriter, and has had much success. But he is not done. In what is an excellent love kiss to the school, the region, and the kinds of music it produced, Richie has given us what I think is the CD of 2012, *Tuskegee*.

***

I know personally, if I knew little about someone like Booker T. Washington, I would want to know more, and this book would be a great place to start.

Amy Jacques Garvey: Selected Writing from the Negro World, 1923-1928

Edited by Louis J. Parascandola

Reviewed by Fred Beauford

A Wonderful Mind

Amy J, Garvey, an obscure figure for most Americans, was the second wife of the famous Black Nationalist leader Marcus Garvey. Garvey, an immigrant from Jamaica, "created the most significant black mass movement in history. His organization, the Universal Negro Improvement Association and African Communities (UNIA) was first established in Jamaica in 1914."

As Parascandola also notes in his introduction, after Garvey came to the United States in 1916, "by the early 1920s, he had created more than 900 branches in some 40 countries with about 6 million members. UNIA was a pro-capitalist, masculine movement that promoted race pride, Pan African unity, economic self-sufficiency, and the redemption of Africa from European imperial power.'"

Amy Jacques Garvey shared this vision with the same passion as her husband. However, soon after they married, Marcus Garvey started freefalling from grace. First, he came under attack from establishment blacks. Some, like the august W.E.B. Du Bois, thought that he had little understanding of American blacks, and worse, that he was crude, with little class.

Others, like A. Philip Randolph, loved Marxism with the same, blinding passion that the Garveys loved capitalism. This is what Amy Garvey wrote in the *Negro World*, as she and Marcus made a cross-country train trip, stopping at big and small cities where they had branches of their organization:

"A town or city exists on nothing. Its backbone is either the minerals of the earth or the vegetation of the fields. Either manufacturing or farming, and in both cases handling and distribution play an important part. In cases of seaport towns and big railroad centers, distribution of goods of all kinds is an industry in itself. Where are our big thinkers who are laying an industrial foundation to save us from economic starvation? We have none."

In addition to the black socialists, who would have none of this, there were the whites that also became alarmed by her husband's separatist views and his growing influence in black communities nationwide.

Writes Parascandola, "Under fire from all of these groups, particularly after Garvey's meeting with the Ku Klux Klan in 1922 to discuss matters of racial separation, the movement began to collapse. Garvey came under indictment on charges of mail fraud involving the Black Star Line stock in 1922, was convicted in 1923, imprisoned in 1925, and was eventually deported in 1927. It was during this turbulent time that Amy Jacques Garvey became involved in UNIA and the *Negro World*," the weekly newspaper that Marcus Garvey founded in America, in addition to the Black Star Steamship Line, restaurants, laundries, a hotel, a printing press and a doll factory.

Amy Garvey met her husband in 1919 and became his personal secretary. She was born in Kingston, Jamaica, to a middle-class family, was mixed race and well educated at an elite Jamaican school. She moved to New York City in 1917, and, despite her own racially mixed background, quickly became influenced by Garvey's idea that "God had deliberately created the races differently and intended them to be separated."

She was put in charge of the Woman's Pages of the *Negro World,* but what she wrote was not something I would have read in most woman pages in newspapers and magazines across the country during this period, no matter what the color or creed.

First, the entire newspaper was printed in Spanish, English and French, reflecting a worldview. Second, her essays, editorials and occasional short fiction reflected this worldview. You have already read some of her thoughts on the virtue of capitalism, which showed us an excellent grasp of large-scale production and distribution of goods. In addition, she also had a firm grasp of international issues.

Amy Garvey commented on events happening in Asia, Europe, Africa and the Middle East, even predicting that one day the "Yellowman," as it were, will one day rule the earth.

She also kept a sharp eye on Gandhi and applauded his efforts to end the practice of the English strategy of divide and conquer by telling Hindus, Muslims, Sikhs, Jainists, Buddhists, Zoroastrians and pockets of Christians and Jews, that in the end, they were all Indians and that the English should go back to where they came from.

Amy Garvey was also a strong feminist. Here is an excerpt from one of her essays on the subject: "There is nothing more significant in the life of mankind than the gradual emancipation of woman from her dependence upon man and the giving to her a decisive voice in her relations to man in the family."

She goes on in the same article to praise Mustapha Kemal, who had just liberated Turkey from centuries of rule by Islamic sultans, "for a more honorable place for woman." As for America, she predicted that in a "few decades I would not be surprised to see a woman President."

This obviously didn't happen, nor did quite a few of her other predictions. Nevertheless, this was a person with an excellent mind who didn't mind using it. Editor Parascandola noted that although she was a prolific writer and original thinker, she has been grossly overlooked by history.

Most of the reason, he writes, is because "she often deflected attention from herself to her husband," Marcus Garvey.

Hopefully, this historic book will finally give her her due.

Too Smart for His Own Good
Malcolm X: A Life of Reinvention

by Manning Marable
Reviewed by Fred Beauford

"To be a Negro living in America, and to be consciously aware, is to be in a state of constant outrage." James Baldwin

As I look back on the history of this country, no one fits Baldwin's observation better than Malcolm Little (aka Malcolm X).

As he slowly emerges in Manning Marable's sometimes overwhelming, richly researched, 594-page book, Malcolm is an often-perplexing combination of incredibly high intelligence, abject ignorance, a profound awareness and an unbending anger at America's mistreatment of blacks; all of which guides him, and tears him apart, leading him to become one of the most famous of Americans, the angry, revenge seeking Malcolm X.

The seeds for this transformation, which Professor Marable outlines with considerable skill and scholarship—were planted early.

Both of Malcolm's parents were dedicated followers of the Jamaican immigrant, Marcus Garvey. Professor Marable points out that Garvey and his followers believed that "Racial separation...was essential...people of African descent were all part of a transnational 'nation.' A global race with a common destiny."

This was during the time that one of the greatest human migrations in modern history was set into motion, as blacks started fleeing the fascist South, first in small trickles, and then in droves, in search of the democracy they had heard so much about.

Also, something just as motivating and whose importance continues until this day, was buried deep in Malcolm's parents' psyche, as well as most African Americans:

Who am I? Who was I before I was dragged unwillingly to this horrendous place called America?

Newly formed black communities in the urban North, in cities like Detroit, New York's Harlem, Cleveland and Chicago, were rife with exploitative religious charlatans and deeply sincere individuals like Garvey, all with the same compelling answer to the confused blacks trying mightily to find an answer to the two tormenting, overwhelming ideas that constantly haunted them: you are not who the slave master said you were and here is who you really are.

Malcolm's father, Earl Little, and his second wife Louise, Malcolm's mother, threw themselves into Garvey's organization, the Universal Negro Improvement Association (UNIA).

***

Malcolm's mother grew up in St. Andrew, Grenada. His dark-skinned, American born father lived most of his life in the Great Lakes region, the Midwest and even Canada, where he first met Malcolm's mother.

"Unlike Earl," writes Marable, "she had received an excellent Anglican elementary-level education, becoming a capable writer as well as fluent in French...had a fair complexion and dark, flowing hair; in everyday encounters she was often mistaken for white."

Despite such strong differences in background and physical appearances, what united them was a passionate commitment to Garvey's famous dictum: "Up you mighty race. You can be what you will!"

Misfortune soon overwhelmed Malcolm's family, however, and the bare outline of what happened next has been well documented, with additional, tantalizing and controversial nuggets sprinkled throughout the narrative of Professor Marable's biography.

After the suspicious death of his father, his mother confined to a mental hospital, foster homes, crime, jail; and ultimately, the Nation of Islam, led by Elijah Muhammad, Malcolm Little finally becomes Malcolm X.

It was here, as a young, uneducated man in his twenties, that his barely noticed towering intellect, and his inner self-discipline, came to center stage. As an organizer, public speaker and debater, Malcolm X excelled and began to attract much attention, including that of local police, as well as the Feds, and he soon was watched wherever he went.

Although he knew the FBI was on his tail, this did nothing to deter him, and he kept up a punishing schedule, traveling to Los Angeles, to Detroit, to Chicago, and to Boston, all the while serving as the minister of the Harlem temple.

Marable points out that, "Although Malcolm usually spoke at Muslim temples (later called mosques after growing heat from orthodox Islam) his audiences increasingly consisted of both Muslim and non-Muslim blacks. In his language and style, Malcolm reached out to recruit black Christians to his cause."

His growing popularity "generated a financial windfall for the Nation. Between five hundred and one thousand African Americans were joining almost every month...much of the new revenue went into commercial ventures...the economic success of these ventures may have been responsible for Elijah Muhammad's decision to stop mentioning some of the original tenets of Wallace D. Fard's Islam—in particular the bizarre Yacub's history—and give greater emphasis to the Garveyite thesis that a self-sustainable, all-black capitalist economy was a viable strategy," writes Professor Marable.

Malcolm X was blessed with a trademark "bitter wit," and was a powerful public speaker (How many books I have read that pointed out that the real history of us humans is how we react to the spoken word. It seems that the speech is mightier than the pen, or the sword).

Media and universities, including Howard, Cornell and Harvard soon sought him out to speak before students and faculty, or to provide a quote. This interest was fueled by the very real drama of the growing Civil Rights Movement in the South.

They all knew by now, that Malcolm was a great orator, and a provocative and confident lecturer.

Combined with the television screen suddenly being filled with brilliant black thinkers like James Baldwin, Bayard Ruskin, and now this guy who called himself Malcolm X, it provided an interesting, intellectual public face to the African American struggle, with more than merely black clerics from the south having visibility and the only voice.

It is easy to see, in the 20/20 hindsight of history, why he was in such demand.

Malcolm X would perhaps turn over in his grave at my reference to his being an intellectual, but how else to account for the rapid learning experiences he had to face and master, time after time?

Herb Boyd points out, in his insightful review of the book in the *Amsterdam News,* that "It wasn't a reinvention; rather an evolution."

***

You hardcore eggheads out there reading this, please hold your nose, and forgive me, but reading this book brought back to mind an old *Star Trek* episode. In it, Captain Kirk is put on a strange planet, the likes of which he had rarely encountered, with a far greater physical reptilian adversary, by forces unknown.

The unknowns explained to both of them that everything they needed to defeat one another was right in front of them.

Captain Kirk, as well as Malcolm X, were both forced to quickly make use of whatever they found immediately around them; and their intelligence, and quick thinking were their main weapons against their opponents.

Kirk survived because of his intensive back knowledge, and even sternly lectured the powerful unknowns who had placed him there in the first place.

For Malcolm X, we all know what happened next. He did not survive, because he had little back knowledge when he embarked upon a journey that made him one of the most recognizable names to come out of the long struggle for freedom for African Americans.

He had to learn everything he needed to rise to such heights, as he went along in his remarkable journey.

His early ignorance, in spite of his being smart, ultimately caused jealousy and hatred and leading him down and trapped in a world that finally caught up with him, and bit him.

To me, this explains Malcolm X, and why, in the end, he just may have been too smart for his own good.

***

Another note concerning Malcolm X: Gene Roberts, the undercover NYPD officer that had infiltrated his organization and tried to revive him after he was shot down before his wife and children, was once a friend of mine, and one of the few black students at Olinville Junior High, and grew up near me in the Gunhill Houses.

***

Professor Manning Marable, a longtime member of the faculty of Columbia University, died the same day that his book, *Malcolm X: A Life of Reinvention* was released.

We all must go sometime, but I can't think of a better way to do it. This is a great book.

The March on Washington: Jobs, Freedom and the Forgotten History of Civil Rights

By William P. Jones

Reviewed by Fred Beauford

The Birth of American Democracy

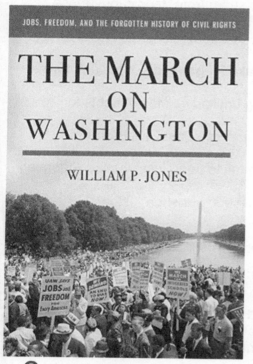

On August 28, 1963 something truly amazing occurred: the birth of true

democracy came to our shores for the very first time. Martin Luther King

Jr.'s famous "I Have a Dream " speech resonated throughout the land, and

as his companion in the fight for Democracy, Ralph Abernathy wrote in his

excellent memoir of the same name, "The Walls Came Tumbling Down."

Although It wasn't King's speech alone that caused the onrush of freedom for women, gays, the crusade for the planet earth to be saved from human greed, and often overlooked, the rights of freedom of movement for the elderly, and folks who suffer from handicaps (those kneeling buses, indented sidewalks and accommodations on public transportation for wheelchairs we now take for granted in cites and towns across the nation, didn't come into being until advocates of rights for freedom of movement started using the tactics of the Civil Rights Movement)—it brilliantly summed up, for all to hear, just what an American democracy should look like for the first time in our short history.

As William P. Jones asserts in his book *The March on Washington: Jobs, Freedom, and the Forgotten History of Civil Rights,* Dr. King, the father of the Civil Rights Movement had many grandfathers and grandmothers, both black and white, and many great-grandparents, for that matter.

One of the grandest grandfathers of all was the towering trade union leader A. Philip Randolph, who founded the Brotherhood of Sleeping

Car Porters, who first called for a march on Washington in 1941 to press for equal opportunity in employment and the armed forces.

Professor Jones, who teaches history at the University of Wisconsin, Madison, first takes us through the volatile radical politics of '30s. For reasons unknown, the '60s always grabbed the headlines for American radicalism, but that decade pales in comparison beside the '30s, the decade Randolph earned his stripes.

Because of the Great Depression, starting with the collapse of Wall Street in 1929, the fun years of the "roaring twenties," with its blazing stock market, jazz and endless booze, dancing and sex, was over.

Now, outright fascism, communism, socialism, anarchism, and racism ruled the streets. Meanwhile, the old establishment dug in, ready for a fight.

What I found most interesting about this decade, with its many problems, with its many politicizing, polarizing ideas, was that so many highly intelligent, educated people, black and white, most with advanced degrees from major universities, decided to use that education and intelligence not to pursue personal wealth, but to try and bring about a better world without regimentation and violence.

Those who were successful, like Randolph, learned to take what they could, and two-stepped around all the rest of the hardcore isms, and keep their eyes on what was truly important: turning America into a true democracy.

Professor Jones takes us on a historical journey that I have been down many times, as the history of the Civil Rights Movement slowly unfolds. What I like most about this narrative, which differs from many I have read, is the credit he gives to Randolph, and especially Bayard Rustin.

The importance of Rustin cannot be overstated. When he first met Dr. Martin Luther King Jr., the young King was leading the Montgomery Bus Boycott, the first civil rights demonstration that gained national attention due to a large measure of the increasing importance of television. This was augmented by the growing threat of unspeakable violence breaking out as blacks started arming themselves in light of the bombings and daily threats directed against them.

Even Dr. King, and Rev. Abernathy requested permits to carry pistols. "I will never forget those threatening telephone calls and letters of intimidation," Abernathy wrote two years later.

Writes Jones, "The escalation of violence caught the attention of A. Philip Randolph…and soon after the bombings a small group of civil rights and labor leaders assembled to discuss the problem in New York City…. Fearing that open warfare would bring a wave of repression far greater than they had seen already, Randolph and the others resolved to send Bayard Rustin to hold a series of workshops on Gandhian nonviolence in Montgomery.

"Despite King's emphasis on nonviolence and his familiarity with Gandhi, Rustin found that the minister had 'very limited notions about how a nonviolent protest should be carried out.' " Writing about his experience years later, Rustin recalled, " 'I do not believe that one does honor to Dr. King by assuming that, somehow, he had been prepared for his job….The glorious thing is that he came to a profoundly deep understanding of nonviolence through the struggle itself, and through reading and discussions which he had in the process of carrying on the protests.' "

In addition to introducing King to the leading black activist intellectual in America at the time, Randolph also offered him more down to earth help by putting him in touch with black union activists in Birmingham, who helped raise funds to send to Montgomery.

I thought a great deal about Rustin sitting alone with King at his dinner table, late into the night, in a polarized Southern city, with the very real threat of a bomb loudly bursting into their quiet space at any moment, instructing King in what Gandhi was trying to tell us about how nonviolence resistance weakens the oppressor until he realizes that he has no moral grounds to stand on.

All I could think of what is happening in the Mideast as I write this. Where is a Rustin when we need one?

***

Randolph's gambit paid off, as a brilliant Rustin made sure that King fully understood what it meant when he invoked the name of Gandhi.

***

One final point, and one that drives be crazy each time I read a book like this. Professor Jones makes the same historic mistake that I have tried to correct for decades: W.E.B. DuBois did not found the NAACP.

Mary White Ovington did, and she is perhaps the greatest unsung heroine in American history.

Here is the true story:

The Springfield Race Riot of 1908 was a mass civil disturbance in Springfield, Illinois, sparked by the transfer of two African American prisoners out of the city jail by the county sheriff. This act enraged many white citizens, who responded by rioting in black neighborhoods, destroying and burning black-owned businesses and homes, and killing black citizens.

By the end of the riot, there were at least seven deaths and $200,000 in property damage. It was the only riot against blacks in United States history in which more white deaths (five) were recorded than black (two). The riot led to the formation of the National Association for the Advancement of Colored People, an organization to work for civil rights, education and improving relations, between blacks and whites.

Ovington, a New Yorker, was appalled by the violence and destruction of property, no less in Lincoln's hometown, so in 1909 she issued a call to prominent religious and social leaders, including reaching out to Dr. Du Bois, Harvard's first black graduate, who, at the time, was trying to get the organization he founded with Monroe Trotter, The Niagara Movement, off the ground.

The Wikipedia page reads: *The Niagara Movement was a black civil rights organization founded in 1905 by a group led by W.E.B. Du Bois and William Monroe Trotter. It was named for the "mighty current" of change the group wanted to effect and Niagara Falls, the Canadian side of which was where the first meeting took place in July 1905. The Niagara Movement was a call for opposition to racial segregation and disenfranchisement, and it was opposed to policies of accommodation and conciliation promoted by African American leaders such as Booker T. Washington.*

In 1910, a year later after joining Ovington's new interracial organization, Du Bois started *The Crisis* magazine, which became the official publication of the newly minted NAACP, and became one of the most feared magazines in American history.

When I became the editor of *The Crisis* in 1984, only the sixth in its long history, I discovered this hidden history about the central role Mary White Ovington played in creating the most effective civil rights organization America has ever seen.

Let us hope that future books on the history of the civil rights struggle in America give her the same due that Professor Jones gives A. Philip Randolph and Bayard Rustin.

Exhibiting Blackness: African Americans and the American Art Museum
by Bridget R. Cooks

Reviewed by Fred Beauford

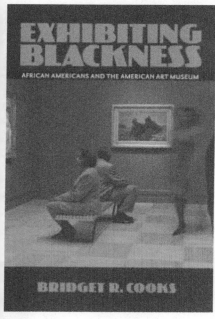

Pity the Poor Visual Artist

The burning question that has intrigued me for most of my adult life is why black musicians, facing the same daunting challenges that native black visual artists, novelists, actors, poets, directors, screenwriters and playwrights, faced— gave the Europeans a swift kick in the butt, and boldly, and loudly, proclaimed themselves King of this, Queen of that, with additional Dukes, Earls, Counts and Princes; and the grand prizes of all, the Queen of Soul, the Queen of the Blues, and the King of Pop.

Talk about giving the finger to folks.

Often unschooled, black musicians, undeterred by racism, and more importantly, unfiltered and unmediated, created the sound track not only for America, but an art form for the entire planet that said "America" more than anything else we have been able to create on these shores.

Not so for the poor, unfortunate creative native blacks who wanted to have the same impact on American culture, but who pursued a career in the visual arts. *Exhibiting Blackness* brings this fact into full focus.

***

I have already given away most of my narrative by the words "unfiltered and unmediated."

***

Writes Professor Bridget R. Cooks, "In 1927, the Chicago Art Institute presented *The Negro in Art Week: Exhibition of Primitive African Sculpture, Modern Paintings, Sculpture, Drawings, Applied Art, and Books*. This was not the first exhibition opportunity for African American artists; however, it marked the first time that an exhibition of art made by African Americans was presented at an art museum."

The exhibition was conceived by the philosopher and cultural leader Professor Alain Locke of Howard University. Locke is regarded as the "Father of the Harlem Renaissance." He, along with W.E.B. Du Bois, was among the first to articulate a clear vision of the use of art, which included literature, dance and the visual arts, as perhaps the major instrument to change the mind of whites that the Negro was "inherently" inferior. He called creative art made by blacks "our first line of defense."

Later, Locke convinced real estate mogul William E. Harmon to establish the Harmon Foundation, which became the most influential organization of the last century to promote and exhibit art made by blacks.

Locke, however, had a vision of what kind of art his "New Negro" was supposed to create, which has had far-reaching consequences. Notes author Cooks, "The desired use value for Negro art exhibitions to have a transformational sociological effect on race relations is a burden that Gary Reynolds, and more recently Mary Ann Calo, have argued was a prominent tension in the interwar period, particularly symptomatic of Harmon Foundation exhibitions. "

The book goes on to list and comment on a number of exhibitions nationwide, including the highly controversial *Harlem on my Mind: Cultural*

Capital of Black America, 1900-1968, sponsored by the Metropolitan Museum of Art in New York City in 1969. In Professor Cooks' lengthy discussion of the many issues surrounding this event, she manages to touch on all the many issues facing black visual artists: are they artist first, or black first? Should their work speak to what being black in a racist society means, or should it speak to more personal demons? And, most importantly, do these one-time exhibitions just give the white world a chance to say, look what we did for you in 1969, with no intention of having black artists shown again in the art institutions they control?

And did they, as the present day publishing industry did to black fiction writers, with their separate, but unequal sections in book stores, as well as separate imprints—marginalize the black visual artist to an unimportant sideshow?

***

I think that history will support my notion that Professor Locke and all the do-gooders, despite good intentions, hopelessly hobbled the creative juices of black writers and visual artists, which continues to this day. Art is not social science and is often not logical.

In the end, no matter what the artistic discipline, to call itself art, it must first connect to a deeply felt core of the artist. It really is that simple; and that core is not always about the other, or the "we." Rather, most commonly, it's about one's self.

That's why we call some folks "artists."

***

On the other hand, black musicians were not culturally deprived of all the lively, low-life honky tonks, the infamous "buckets of bloods," the many greasy spoons and juke joints, where no philosopher or cultural leader, black or white, would dare go if they valued their well-being.

This was their base!

Also, their art was low rent, with little need of well-off patrons of the arts, pointless art critics and society stiffs like Thomas Hoving of the Met, telling them what to do.

Louis Armstrong purchased his first instrument, a cornet, from a pawn shop. In the words of an old bluesman, about his guitar, "If it ain't been in a pawn shop, it can't play the blues."

The amazing music they created, which kept getting better, year after year, reflected this often grim, often profoundly joyful reality; again, using the same words I used before, "unfiltered and unmediated."

And that's how they became the kings and queens of the world.

Who Can Afford to Improvise? James Baldwin and Black Music, the Lyric and the Listeners

By Ed Pavlic

Reviewed by Fred Beauford

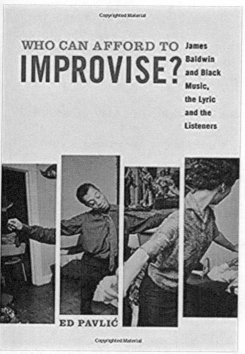

"When it came to people, those in his work, and in his life,

he decided: 'One tries to treat them as the miracles they

are, while trying to protect oneself from the disasters

they've become."

Although this can often be a difficult book for those who do not have a solid, intellectual grounding in novelist-essayist James Baldwin's literary works, it is, nevertheless, an excellent introduction for those who may have heard of him or have only read an essay or two.

Author Ed Pavlic, in *Who Can Afford to Improvise?* offers an amazing, thorough meditation that lets Baldwin do most of the talking. The sense of music in Baldwin's writing, implied in the subtitle, does not fully make the case and takes a decidedly backseat; still, this book is an often-brilliant effort to try to fuse these two different art forms into one.

It is also a fascinating intellectual biography of the man, based on vast amounts of direct quotes from Baldwin's many book reviews, novels, essays, open letters, plays and decades of being interviewed.

***

Baldwin, growing up poor in black Harlem, never stepped foot into a college. He started his career with only a lowly diploma from Dewitt Clinton High School in the Bronx in the late '40s. His first efforts were book reviews for an impressive number of New York City literary and left-wing political magazines. There, his talent as a masterful prose stylist with a deadly, wicked wit quickly became apparent.

Pavlic gives us this from a 1948 review in the *New Leader* of the novel, *The Moth,* by James M. Cain: "The only thing wrong with (Cain's characters) was the fact that they were still reeling from the discovery that they were in possession of visible and functioning sexual organs. It was the impact of this discovery that so hopelessly and murderously disoriented them."

By the time, we get to 1963, after his extraordinary essay, *The Fire Next Time*, was published the year before in *The New Yorker*, Baldwin was arguably the most celebrated writer in America, even making the cover of *Time* magazine.

Here, author Pavlic uses a quote from one of Baldwin's friends, the composer and jazz pianist Alonzo Levister, "When *Fire* came out in *The New Yorker* I was at Horatio Street. He was an overnight star, and I took him to an upscale store, a British American house, for him to buy what I think were the first nice clothes he ever had 'til that time. That's how I remember it."

As the Civil Rights Movement accelerated, the Long Hot Summer of costly black race riots nationwide simmered; the political assassinations of the Kennedys, Malcolm X, and Dr. King occurred; and people of every walk of life came out into the streets in cities and college campuses—now protesting a deeply unpopular Vietnam war. Many in white America turned to Baldwin because he seemed to have predicted all of this with insightful precision in the *Fire Next Time.* It came to life and started scaring them to death.

Also, and just as important for the new national spokesman, now there was the Black Power Movement, which spawned The Black Arts Movement, and the black this and black that.

What was Baldwin now to do? It was becoming increasingly clear to him that he was being thrown increasingly into a powerful maelstrom. Also, he started to have serious doubts about his prose, as brilliant and beautiful as it was. But, in the end, was it of any use, especially for influencing blacks?

Pavlic writes, "As background for the cover story about Baldwin in *Time* magazine (May 17, 1963) Washington correspondent Loyle Miller reported back to the bureau from Harlem, "It is as you suspected: in Harlem, Malcolm X is a man of fame, but James Baldwin was right when he wrote *Nobody Knows My Name.*"

Baldwin had now confronted what every black creative writer in America has always faced, especially the males: who was he writing to? Is it "my fellow countrymen," that Baldwin always addressed with his exceptional prose, or, the blacks of the Harlem he once knew? Could they ever recognize his genius and laud him?

One prominent Harlem leader, former Manhattan borough president and former Malcolm X lawyer, Perry Sutton, poured cold water on that idea. And, said that there was no way that was ever going to happen.

"Baldwin is interesting reading," he said to Miller in 1963, "and, we quote him when he serves our purposes. But, he really has no influence. For one thing, he's difficult reading, so, only the Negro intellectual reads Baldwin, and that severely limits his communication. Remember that Negroes are not influenced by a writer, any writer, because we are not in the main intellectuals. Not enough of us read. The Negroes are influenced by the lecturers, the compelling speakers, the men like Martin Luther King and Malcolm X. When you see him (Baldwin) as a lecturer, you see an effeminate, and that ruins him even with those who have read him. He's a faggot, a fairy. And, we as Negroes have much greater animosity towards lesbians and homosexuals than does the white man, because this is weakness, and there is already too much weakness among Negroes, even among the few that really know about him, and, if he doesn't impress, he can't influence."

Now you can understand why so many black male writers fled America, and why Baldwin died in France. There is a lot to learn in this book.

Conversations with John A. Williams

Edited by Jeffrey Allen Tucker

Reviewed by Fred Beauford

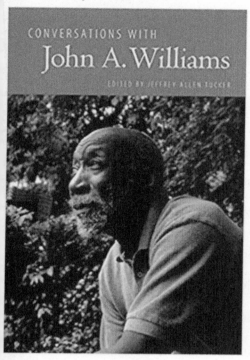

Conversations with Myself

In a way I am reviewing myself because I have one of the conversations

in this book. For me, this marks the third time that one of my conversations

with creative writers have ended up in this series. The other two were

Conversations with Ernest Gaines, and Conversations with Albert Murray.

Both books were published in the '90s.

John A. Williams is one of the most prolific black writers in our history as Americans. His novel, *The Man Who Cried I Am*, and his provocative non-fiction book, *The King God Didn't Save,* became best sellers. In addition, he was written ten other novels, seven volumes of nonfiction, a play, a book of poetry and an opera libretto. He is also one of the least known American writers.

But before I get to him, I want to say a few words about the University Press of Mississippi's Literary Conversation series. The press was founded in 1970 and is supported by Mississippi's eight state universities.

Starting the Literary Conversation series was a stroke of sheer genius by an unknown person I was unable to identify. What I love most about what they have done is how inclusive they've been. Blacks, Jews, Asians, WASPS—the entire American family, including Ishmael Reed, E.L. Doctorow, Maxine Hong Kingston, S.J. Perelman and Anais Nin—are all included. I also like the fact that they market their products to universities and public and private libraries all over the world.

The current Series editor is Monika Gehlawat, Associate Professor of English and Director of Graduate Studies at The University of Southern Mississippi.

Over the years, the press has published more than 1,000 titles and distributed more than 2,600,000 copies worldwide, including the Literary Conversations series. They have given the world a great showcase for American writers, and I am damn glad to know that I can walk into almost any major university and public library in the world and find a book, thanks to them, with one of my articles in it.

Who wouldn't want to be a part of something like that?

***

As I read the interviews in the newest book from the Conversation Series, a few things jumped out at me. One is that Williams was in his novels an unapologetic radical. Over and over he seems to be saying that blacks should pick up the gun and wage war against whites.

One reviewer even asked him if he had ever been "accused of incitement through your writings at all?"

He answered, "Not yet, but I wish I had. I say that with much pride because I would like to feel that my writings were important enough to in many ways influence the course of not only my country's history, my people's history, but the world. I suppose every writer would like to be a

Dostoyevsky, a Dickens, a Balzac, a Herman Melville, and to this end I feel that I failed."

Now I can see why I title my Conversation, *John A. Williams: Agent Provocateur.* Another thing I noticed rereading the essay I wrote as an undergraduate at NYU and published in my first magazine, the now historic arts and letters magazine, *Black Creation*, and many of the other conversations in the book—was how many times he blamed the media for most of the ills facing this country.

I pooh-poohed him in my conversation.

It was 1971 when I wrote it. I was in my senior year at NYU, about to graduate with a degree in journalism. I had launched *Black Creation* a few years prior that and it was now a national magazine. Needless to say, I loved being a journalist.

Little did I know that when I got out into the real world, that this business, that I loved so much, was a racist, sexist, nationalistic, tribal business. There was no such thing as American journalism. All you can do is the best you can, as the tribal and racial leaders gave us little to remind us that there as such a thing as an American.

No wonder there was such loneliness in America. There did not yet exist a narrative.

This was what Williams was trying to tell me in our brief encounter—and I was to find out that his message wasn't pretty.

This book was released with another conversation worth reading, *Conversations with Joan Didion.*

Losing My Cool: How a Father's Love and 15,000 Books Beat Hip-Hop Culture

By Thomas Chatterton Williams

Reviewed by Fred Beauford

Surviving Rap

One of the most devastating attacks

on so-called hip-hop culture I have read

comes not from grumpy old black men

like everyone's favorite father, Bill Cosby,

or from one of the most outspoken critics

of rap, *New York Daily News* columnist

Stanley Crouch, the self-described

"hanging judge," but from someone who

grew up with and once had deeply

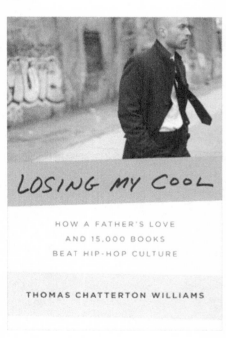

embraced the culture, Thomas Chatterton Williams.

In the end, however, the crux of *Losing My Cool: How a Father's Love and 15,000 Books Beat Hip-Hop Culture*, by the first-time author, is not just about rap...and hip-hop culture, whether Williams realizes it or not, but is also about his trying to define himself as someone from a mixed-race family in a racial climate that determined whether you were either black or white.

Losing My Cool is following in what is emerging as a distinctly American literary genre in its own right: the search for identity of mixed-race Americans, especially African Americans. Williams is walking along a trail already blazed boldly by the outstanding *One Drop: My Father's Hidden Life--A Story of Race and Family Secrets*, by Bliss Broyard, Rebecca Walker's *Black White and Jewish*, James McBride's impressive *The Color of Water*, and, of course, the most famous of them all, the outrageously popular best seller *Dreams From my Father: A Story of Race and Inheritance*, which not only made Barack Obama a very rich man, but quite possibly helped elect him President of the United States.

Williams writes early on in his memoir: "Despite my mother's being white, we were a black and not an interracial family. Both of my parents stressed this distinction and the result was that, growing up, race was not so complicated an issue in our household. My brother and I were black, period.... We were taught from the moment we could understand spoken words that we would be treated by whites as though we were black whether we liked it or not, and so we needed to know how to move in the world as black men. And that was that."

But how does someone who is mixed race, and lives in a mainly white section of his town of Fanwood, New Jersey, become authentic, or keep it "real," a word Williams often uses in this maiden effort?

"One day when I was around nine," he writes, "my mother drove Clarence (his older brother) and me to Unisex Hair Creation, a black barbershop in a working-class section of Plainfield." This is where he encounters a hostile black woman who resents them for driving a used Mercedes-Benz, calling them, "rich, white motherfuckers."

His mother tells him to ignore her. But what he couldn't ignore was the "fake wood-paneled color television suspended from the ceiling" in the barbershop. It was always fixed on one channel, Black Entertainment Television (BET), and the program *Rap City* was on each time he visited, and this fact changed his life.

He notes, "I don't know…that I had ever noticed BET before, and in the strange, homogeneously black setting of Unisex Hair Creation…the sight of this all-black cable station mesmerized and awed me."

"Watching BET felt cheap and even wrong on an intuitive level; Pappy called it minstrelsy—but the men and women in the videos didn't just contend for my attention, they demanded it, and I obliged them. They were so luridly sexual, so gaudily decked out, so physically confident with an oh-I-wish-a-nigga-would air of defiance, so defensively assertive, I couldn't pry my eyes away.

"...I knew for sure the other boys in the shop didn't seem to question any of it, and I sensed that I shouldn't either....I paid attention to the slang they were using and decided I had better learn it myself. Terms like "nigga" and "bitch" were embedded in my thought process, and I was consciously aware for the first time that it wasn't enough just to know the lexicon.... Over the weeks and months that followed, as I became more adept at mimicking and projecting blackness the BET way...what struck me most about this new behavior was how far it veered from my white classmates and friends at Holy Trinity."

Two keys things were happening to the young Williams, and I have written extensively about both of them. In these very pages, I pointed out that I, too, had once been "mesmerized" by the culture of young street blacks that has now mesmerized the entire world. And, like Williams, I gladly abandoned my white world and sunk myself deeply into this exciting world, so I know first hand where the young brother is coming from.

There was something else at work in Williams' world that that did not exist in the world of my youth. In my youthful world, poor street blacks still had everyone's attention, but others spoke for them, whether it was positive or that they wanted to ship them all back to Africa. They were just the voiceless faces, head bowed, being led away to jail in handcuffs each night on the local news.

The electronic revolution slowly, but surely, changed all of that.

In the youthful world Williams inhabited, text was no longer king, unlike the world I grew up in, as the relentless electronic revolution Samuel Morse launched on May 24, 1844, not only gave a voice to the so-called "Brother in the Street," but amplified his voice to the extent that that voice had, in effect, drowned out the other black voices I heard growing up, like the soul touching lyricism of Langston Hughes, the sweet voices of the doo wop groups singing plaintively about love and longing, the sassy eloquence of James Baldwin, the profound intellectualism of W.E.B. Du Bois, and the almost cosmic idealism of Martin Luther King Jr.

Instead, the loudest voices Williams heard that were considered the most authentically black, were the harsh words of rappers. Those voices were about hoes, bitches, sex, guns, booze, drugs and the pitiless hardness of the thug life.

Niggers With Attitude, if you will.

And these young men soon became the envy of young men everywhere in the world, which is why they have made so much money for so many.

In keeping with the in law of unintended consequences, American slavery and the emasculation of the black male, had, in effect, liberated these young men from the constraints that fathers placed on young men everywhere.

There was no need to slay the father, because the father wasn't there. Without fathers breathing down their horny little necks, these young men were able to act out in total abandonment like every hot-blooded young man in the world would love to do.

***

As the years went by, Williams became even more "street," as he finally moved to a school that had a large number of low-income black students.

He learned to be hard, to consider young black girls bitches, as not something to love and protect, but something to use for sex and material gain.

Music, sports, how you dressed, and how you expressed yourself, ruled that world.

Yet something else also lurked powerfully in Williams' background—Pappy. Pappy was a man from the south, who had refused to be emasculated. Not only did he have the nerve to marry a white woman, but he had earned a Ph.D, not because of America, but despite America, and had developed a deep, abiding love of books and education, and was determined to pass this on to his two sons, despite the loud noise of BET and the streets.

Williams notes: "Pappy, no longer working as a sociologist, now put his Ph.D and extensive store of personal knowledge and reading to use running a private academic and SAT preparation service from our home. From the second grade on, giving Pappy our best meant we needed to try hard in school, but more important than that, we needed to study one-on-one with him in the evenings and on the weekends, on long vacations, and all throughout the summer break. If we could not do that, he was able to make our home the most uncomfortable inn to lodge in. When Clarence began blowing off work, he didn't just get grounded, he came home to find his bedroom walls stripped bare, his Michael Jordan and Run-D.M.C. posters replaced with pastel sheets of algebra equations Pappy had printed out and tacked up."

In other words, throughout his high school years, Williams was living a double life: hardcore street on the outside, including once slapping around his girlfriend because she "disrespected" him, and his father's dutiful son on the inside. One gets the sense from *Losing My Cool* that his father knew the inner turmoil that his youngest son was experiencing, and worried deeply about which side would win in the end.

It was only after a dismal first year at Georgetown University, while Williams still trying to have it both ways, that the eureka moment came. On his summer break he really looked at all the books his father owned for the first time. "I had lived in the midst of written treasure for nineteen years somehow without ever having noticed it, I realized that summer, as if the books in our house used to be wrapped in invisible dust jackets or hidden behind mirrors....Startled friends would point them out to me when they came over, timidly, as if they thought Pappy was a sadist and this was his torture chamber."

Part of this awakening came after he found out that his former girlfriend, Stacy, was pregnant. He asked her what the guy who knocked her up did for a living. "'Nigga, he sells crack!' she shrieked."

This sends his mind whirling. "I doubt I would have realized all this that night in the car, but it is true: In the sixty-three years between the moment when my smart grandmother had Pappy at seventeen, embarrassing her family and her church by doing so, and the moment when Stacy got pregnant at the turn of the millennium, becoming too cool for school and embarrassing no one, black life had changed in dramatic ways. Humanism and civil rights were in, hip-hop was in, nihilism was in, self-pity was in, the street was in, and pride and shame were out—two more cultural anachronisms confined to the African American dustbins of history, like jazz music and zoot suits."

A bit of an overstatement, to be sure, brought on by great disappointment; but well said, and Williams goes back to Georgetown a changed man, meets a highly intelligent woman who is also of mixed race, and starts fully embracing smartness for the first time in his life, and does well.

Pappy had clearly beaten the streets, and this fact alone makes this book worth reading. I just wish he had given us more about his mother. Did she play any part in all of this, like James McBride's memorable, fierce, larger than life Jewish mother in *The Color of Water*? By comparison, Williams' mother is a mere shadow in this book.

***

Rap Moguls Russell Simmons and Sean Combs made millions, and Robert Johnson, founder of BET, became America's first black billionaire, convincing young black men that the thug life was keeping it real. In the end, thanks to Pappy, Williams found out that this was a big lie designed to enrich a few by giving the youth of the world an easy, entertaining way to live out their fantasies.

Now that jails are filled with the young African American men the rap moguls inspired, I hope they choke on their ill-gotten gains. When all is said and done, they have nothing to be proud of. I also hope by some slim chance they read Losing *My Cool: How a Father's Love and 15,000 Books Beat Hip-Hop Culture* to see at what cost they made their princely fortunes.

Is Marriage for White People?
by Ralph Richard Banks

Reviewed by Fred Beauford

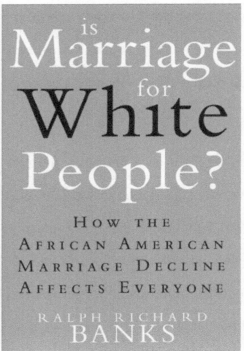

Truths Told and Truths Untold

What is most interesting about reading books about the many problems still facing American blacks, is that the truths told are never quite as interesting as the truths untold. This book is a perfect example.

First the truths told. Marriage as an institution has virtually collapsed for African Americans. As Ralph Richard Banks, a law professor at Stanford University, writes in *Is Marriage for White People?* "The African American [marriage] decline is not limited to the poor. It now encompasses the middle and upper-middle class. Indeed, by some measures the racial gap in marriage is actually wider among the prosperous than among the impoverished."

Professor Banks concentrates his book on interviews with middle class black women, who he says are the most likely to be unwed of any group in the country (although I have read, and heard on television, many sources claim that the women in America most likely to never marry, or have children, are Jewish, followed by college educated African American women), contrasting them with their white counterparts, with only a passing nod to Hispanics and Asians.

But before he gets to his interviews, he offers us a brief look at what caused this great decline in marriage, which accelerated in the late '60s and early '70s. Under a section he entitles "Partial Explanation," Professor Banks lists the destructive effects of slavery and African culture. "The idea here," he explains, "is that the African societies from which the slaves were taken featured extended family structures in which marriage was less pivotal...the African culture explanation became popular during the 1970s."

He also cites de-industrialization, which has made so many black men unmarriageable and the criminalization of black males because of the so-called "War on Drugs."

As his Partial Explanation headline suggests, Professor Banks "partially" dismisses these theories. This is my first major disagreement with him. The attempt is to boldly affirm the African influence in America, and especially on African American culture, had a profound impact. This influence was reinforced by the rise of Black Studies Departments and programs at almost every college and university where there were black students, and where Cultural Nationalism held considerable sway.

As a cultural editor during the Black Consciousness Movement, from 1968 to 1974, when black Cultural Nationalism was in its heyday, what I heard over and over from the speakers I covered, and much of what I published in my magazine, *Black Creation*, was that black people needed to throw off white middle class values, and that included idea of the nuclear family.

The black middle class was mocked by poets like Amiri Baraka, then Leroi Jones, and Howard Professor Nathan Hare, and countless others as being nothing but "black Anglo-Saxons." Sellouts, race traitors, which caused my former colleague, UC Berkeley Professor William Banks, to wonder in his insightful book *Black Intellectuals,* how anyone could attack this small group of hard-working folks who were succeeding not because of what America had to offer, but *despite* what America offered to its black citizens.

In retrospect, the Black Consciousness Movement was a conservative backlash to forces unleashed by the successes of the Civil Rights Movement: racist signs were taken down; whites could actually now go to jail for harming a black; more blacks were flocking to major universities; blacks could get a job at former racist institutions like CBS, for example, and live in any neighborhood they could afford.

And a black man in America could, for the first time in 377 years, date whomever he pleased.

***

The late '60s, and early '70s saw a dramatic, highly noted rise in dating between white women and black men. By sharp contrast, the more than noticeable partnering today of white men and Asian woman has hardly produced a yawn, unlike the mass hysteria of the early '70s caused by newly liberated, happy, gallivanting black men and white woman running amok in joyful partnering.

Feminist leader Gloria Steinem knew just how to piss off and intimidate white men in power when she showed up in *Newsweek,* at the start of the

Women's Liberation Movement, with her boyfriend, the very dark, handsome, well-sculpted, black Olympic star Rafer Johnson.

This sudden freedom is what caused the conservative backlash. Black clerics saw empty churches, and loss of control over their "flock;" politicians and civil rights leaders saw a loss of power and a shrinking base and black women saw their worst nightmare—black men and white women carrying on in public, right before their eyes.

The end result was that black cultural nationalists teamed up with liberals, who also feared assimilation, and demonized and made integration a hateful word, and recreated "separate but equal" as best they could, now known as diversity.

***

Professor Banks spends a great deal of time in his book on the subject of interracial dating, noting that black women are the least likely to date someone of another race than any other group in the country, and, as he points out, given the fact that black women now have more money and more education than black men, is it any wonder that so many will never marry?

Still, those nagging articles about Jewish women not marrying in numbers greater than blacks, and a male Jewish population, among the most highly educated and prosperous in the nation, more than holding their own with Jewish women, made me think that maybe there was something else at play.

***

As I read *Is Marriage for White People?* I started to wonder if Professor Banks would ever get to some untold truths. I was just about to give up on him when near the end of his book, on page 165, he delivers: "The anxiety that black women feel about having biracial children may have been exacerbated by social and cultural changes that we rightly regard as progress. For most of American history, the question of whether a black woman's children would be black was a nonstarter…that was done by the so-called one drop rule…according to this principle, reflected in social practice and law alike, one drop of black blood was sufficient to make a person black. In the infamous 1896 case of Plessey v. Ferguson, for example, the fact that seven out of Homer Plessey's eight great-grandfathers were white was not sufficient to allow him to sit in the white railroad car in segregated Louisiana.

"Now the relaxation of that coercive system means that children with one black parent and one white parent will have unprecedented freedom to define their own racial identity. The same freedom that allows people to fashion their own identity compounds the anxiety of African Americans in particular, who worry that if people can exit, perhaps they will."

***

The English settlers invented the one drop rule so that they could hold their mixed race offspring in bondage, as Thomas Jefferson did, and enforced that rule at the point of a gun, and later, in the Supreme Court, as Professor Banks so aptly points out.

What the Professor didn't do, however, was to complete the untold truth, and draw the logical conclusion that African Americans are not a race in the sense that we know Africans and Europeans to be, but are a multi-racial ethnic group, and there have always been racial differences within this group that were long suppressed by the ruthless oppression of the Northern European settlers, that came pouring out at the success of the Civil Rights Movement.

The biggest mistake the black cultural nationalists made, and continue to make, which greatly contributes to so many educated black men running away from commitment, is that they made marrying a black woman, the darker the better, a political obligation, ruining everything.

My first wife, the mother of two of my four children, was dark brown, and had a beautiful face and a nice big round behind. I loved kissing her full lips. She was not my awesome black African queen, or my strong black sister. She was simply a beautiful woman, and I was damn glad that she was my wife.

Perhaps marrying someone because they had a nice ass and big, soft lips was not the smartest thing in the world to do, but it contained more genuine emotional content than marrying someone out of guilt, or just to make a political statement.

And, instead of sitting around night after night, discussing race, my wife and I made babies.

American Presidents and Notable

Andrew Johnson
by Annette Gordon-Reed

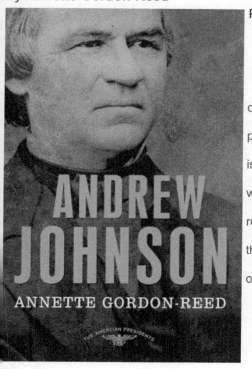

Reviewed by Fred Beauford

For years, I have had my own versions

of heaven and hell. They are both the same

place, centered in the same spirit world that

is all around us. However, in this incredible

world, if you can call it that (because I don't

really have the words yet to fully describe it),

there are no sweet and willing young virgins,

or costumed clerics strutting about and

pulling rank, all the while claiming to be close friends of the Committee of Four, the real Almighties.

Or even, for that matter, free fried chicken joints!

In this world, even the sex-seeking dullards come fully alive, because it offers wonder after wonder that even the most insightful of us, on that blessed place we once called earth, never came close to getting right. We humans just didn't have the information that we needed to see things that can only vaguely be conceived of as earth-bound, carbon-based creatures, totally unaware of all that surrounds us

Those that went to heaven were free to explore this vast, wondrous universe, and if they were diligent enough, thoughtful enough and curious enough--as they floated blissfully by in total wonderment--they might finally learn what their true purpose truly was.

***

Those who committed gross crimes against life, the most precious element in the universe (because that's what fuels it, and gives it purpose) were forced to face the descendants of those they had wronged, as long as their descendants still lived on Earth, or whatever world they were from.

For example, my favorite American arch villain, Thomas Jefferson, would have to stand and face eons of African Americans, even those with just one drop of decadency—of all sizes, shapes and colors (including some of his own close relatives), where they could walk up to him and utter one word: "Parasite," and force him to bow down, as one by one, they slapped him in the face on their way to their own heaven or hell.

For President Andrew Johnson, who the U.S. had the misfortune to be the person to succeed the slain Lincoln, his hell would be to have to sit alone in a hot, humid, lonely, gloomy log cabin, much like the old south he knew well, and read and reread, until he once again collapsed back into the cosmic egg—Harvard professor Annette Gordon-Reed's biography of him.

As an old Southern expression goes, "she laid some serious wood on him."

Gordon-Reed writes, comparing President Abraham Lincoln to Vice President Andrew Johnson: "But what made the difference between them? Why was Lincoln the right man at the right time? Why did Johnson fail so miserably when fate handed him the reins of power? Lincoln tops almost every list of the greatest American presidents, admired by conservatives and liberals alike. Johnson, on the other hand, is almost always found among the worst, if not *the* worst—the man who botched Reconstruction, who energized and gave aid and comfort to the recently defeated enemies of the United States, the first president to be impeached by the House of Representatives, escaping by a hairsbreadth, one vote, in the Senate. America went from the best to the worst in one presidential term."

She couldn't have made her point clearer.

She also points out that Johnson was no friend to blacks: "Throughout the entirety of his political career Andrew Johnson did everything he could to make sure blacks would never become equal citizens in the United States of America. Tragically, he was able to bring the full force and prestige of the American presidency to the efforts."

I was already well aware of Johnson's betrayal of Lincoln, the newly freed black slaves, and all of those 600,000 Americans that had perished in the war before I started reading this book. Perhaps that is why what I found most intriguing about this story, written by a Pulitzer Prize-winning author, is how a poor, uneducated person--poor white trash, if you will--who was born in circumstances just a short rung above the blacks slaves he came to hate so profoundly, managed to claw his way to the most powerful position the New World had to offer. Up until this point in American history, high-level politicians from the south, in Johnson's case, Tennessee, were all from the elite, slave-owning class.

This is where Gordon-Reed clearly excels as a writer and historian. Despite her obvious antipathy toward Andrew Johnson, she allows his story to be told. This is the first time I can remember being treated to such a full-bodied treatment of the prototype of a Southern white male, who was left out of the grand feast that was slavery, and who despised the planter class and the black slaves, because of it.

In commenting on Johnson's hard-scrabble life as the son of parents without property, whose father died when he was just a small child, and who had to enter into a binding apprenticeship to the local tailor at the age of ten (until he ran away from him at the age of fifteen), Gordon-Reed notes, "We can never be certain, but it was probably during these early years that Andrew Johnson began to develop his deep-seated obsession with the wrongs that poor whites suffered at the hands of the planter class and their alleged enslaved co-conspirators. In Johnson's later formulation, slavery was not primarily the destroyer of black lives. Its chief harm was that it prevented lower-class whites from rising to take their rightful place at the head of the table…as his action during his presidency suggest, Johnson's much-vaunted hatred of the southern planter class was born of deep envy and a form of unrequited admiration."

On his own from fifteen, Andrew Johnson nevertheless rose from successful businessman to alderman, state senator, congressman, governor, senator and finally, to vice president in Lincoln's second term. This ascendency arose from someone who only learned to read in his early twenties.

Professor Gordon-Reed points out that much of his success was due to the fact that he was a powerful public speaker, steadfast in his defense of whites left out of the spoils of slavery, as well as a bombastic, plain-spoken bully. What brought him to the attention of President Lincoln was his long, consistent defense of the Union, and his later out-spoken opposition to slavery, although he once supported the "peculiar Institution."

"…nearing the end of his first term," she writes, "Abraham Lincoln, one of the most brilliant politicians in American history, was in trouble. He was facing challenges within his own party and from a growing peace movement fueled by…war weariness. Lincoln needed a running mate who could send a clear statement of his resolve to see the war through to a successful end, even as he tried to lay the groundwork for reconciliation between North and the South. Who better to do this than a 'War Democrat' from one of the rebel states?"

Johnson faced great personal and political damage in the South because of his stance. Although most of Tennessee joined the new Confederacy, he was the only Southern senator who remained in the U. S. Senate, and using all of his gifted skills as an orator, spoke out forcefully against secession, which, as Professor Gordon-Reed points out, greatly endeared him to Northerners, and the abolition movement, although the great Frederick Douglass is quoted early in the book that he felt that Johnson was "no friend to blacks."

Was this why Lincoln, committing perhaps the biggest mistake in his political career, just to get re-elected, dumped his previous vice president, Hannibal Hamlin, and picked Johnson? Professor Gordon-Reed hedges her bets, though the evidence she presents certainly makes that case.

For those who do not know that much about the details of what happened next, which led to the unrest that we faced for much of the 20th century, this is good book with which to start.

Mark Twain and the Colonel: Samuel L. Clemens, Theodore Roosevelt and the Arrival of a New Century

By Philip McFarland

Reviewed by Fred Beauford

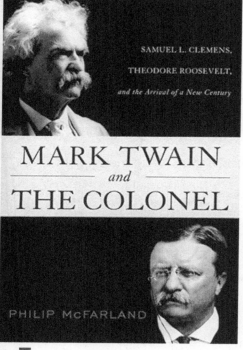

This was a sometimes difficult book for me to firmly get a grip on,

mainly because something deep inside of me felt the pairing of Samuel L.

Clemens (Mark Twain) and Theodore Roosevelt in a book was odd,

indeed.

Roosevelt, although considered by historians as one of America's greatest presidents, for most of his life was a bombastic, bellicose war mongering imperialist. This was somewhat tempered by his progressive stand as president to protect wilderness areas, and curb the power of large corporations (called "trusts"). He also passed laws such as The Meat Inspection Act in 1906 and The Pure Food and Drug Act. The Meat Inspection Act of 1906 banned misleading labels and preservatives that contained harmful chemicals. The Pure Food and Drug Act banned food and drugs that were impure or falsely labeled from being made, sold and shipped.

Still, he was someone who killed hundreds of animals for sport, where Clemens was appalled that anyone would kill just for killing's sake, and not for the meat. Roosevelt also reveled in the Spanish American War, where he became a national hero for his exploits at San Juan Hill in Cuba. He later referred to that war, which cost Spain its last two colonies in the New World, Puerto Rico and Cuba, as well as the Philippines—as a "splendid little war."

Clemens, on the other hand, wanted no part of the Civil War, although he was highly sought after by both North and South because of his prized skill as a pilot on the Mississippi River. He sat the entire war out on the West Coast, where his writing career began in earnest.

What both men have in common, however, and the reason why McFarland married the two in his book, is that both were perhaps the most well-known and influential people during this crucial time in America history.

In the last decade of the 19th Century, and the first decade of the 20th century, our modern nation was formed. Writes McFarland, "An agrarian union of states from before the Civil War had given way to a post-bellum industrialized nation. In 1893, the frontier was pronounced closed. In 1896, the Supreme Court decreed that in effect relations between the two races, black and white, were to be kept socially separated—a decision that stood until 1954; remnants of that iniquity litter our lives still. In 1898, we fought a war that transformed the nation abruptly into a world power and made Roosevelt a national hero at age thirty-nine. In 1901, that hero was elevated to President of the United States."

Vice President Theodore Roosevelt became, at 42, the youngest President ever, after the assassination of President McKinley in 1901, only a short time into his second term.

Mark Twain and The Colonel alternates between the lives lived by Clemens and that of Roosevelt, giving the reader an in-depth portrait of the ups and downs of both men's careers and personal lives.

As always, when reading a book about this time in human history, one is once again stuck by just how delicate life was back then. McFarland's book is filled with great physical suffering and untimely deaths. No one, young or old, was spared.

Modern medicine, as we know it today, was barely in its infancy, and money and being well born hardly protected anyone from a sudden, painful attack of something that could kill them, or at the very least, make them wish they were already dead.

***

At the end of a highly eventful life, Clemens was noted for wandering the streets, wherever he was, in all kinds of weather, in an all-white suit, with a huge crop of white hair, and his trademark bushy mustache, glad to be recognized as the international literary lion he had become.

Roosevelt, on the other hand, came to deeply regret his lifelong cheerleading of the so-called "art of war," as he witnessed the wanton slaughter of human life brought on by the carnage of World War I.

No splendid little war here.

This slaughter was brought home in a deeply personal way when his son, Quentin, a daring pilot with the American forces in France, was shot down behind German lines in 1918. Quentin was his youngest son and probably his favorite. It is said the death of his son distressed him so much that Roosevelt never recovered from his loss. Another of his sons, Ted, was also wounded in that conflict.

Roosevelt died a year later in 1919, at the then old age of 60, profoundly chastened.

"The Old Lion is dead," is what his son Archie telegraphed his siblings upon hearing of the death of his father.

The Hiltons: The True Story of an American Dynasty

By J. Randy Taraborrelli

Reviewed by Fred Beauford

My Goodness!

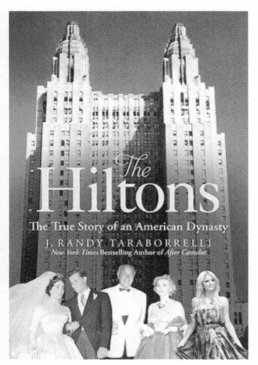

*T*he Hiltons: The True Story of an American Dynasty could just have

easily been entitled, *Conrad Hilton, Zsa Zsa Gabor and the Rise of*

Celebrity Culture. Although the book is a hefty 541 pages, the author, J.

Randy Taraborrelli, is blessed with the deeply invasive skills of the gossip

columnist—a journalistic world where it all hangs out, with little pity for the

subject at hand. And he is also blessed with the equally prying, but far less

flamboyant, more the detached intellectual's fly on the wall, but someone

still looking, unwelcomed, into dark, hidden corridors where well-kept family

secrets are closely held.

The writer makes great use of such a rare gift in this book, so it is hard

to resist, and it held my interest for the entire time.

***

As any student of American journalism well knows, the Hiltons were one

of the first A list celebrities that dominated the society pages in newspapers

and magazines all across America during the '50s. The large regionals and

big cities dailies especially feasted on the comings and goings of society

folks like the Hiltons in Los Angeles, and Babe Paley and Slim Keith in New

York City.

If fact, it can be argued, from reading this book, that Conrad Hilton invented the A List. His second wife, the brown-haired Hungarian-Jewish immigrant, Sari Gabor, who soon after arriving in America quickly became the blonde "ravishing" Zsa Zsa Gabor understood the phenomenon immediately.

During much of the '50s, the sophisticated, witty Zsa Zsa Gabor, now the ex-Mrs. Conrad Hilton, was everywhere on the new medium of television. If Conrad did indeed help invent the A list, certainly Zsa Zsa had a large hand in inventing the moronic rackety yak television talk shows.

As one early critic noted: "She (Gabor) can say nothing in an entertaining way better that anyone else."

Conrad's oldest son, the handsome, tragic, alcoholic, hot tempered, insecure "playboy" Nicky Hilton, who died at the age of 49, was the Paris Hilton of his day, being followed by reporters everywhere.

No wonder. He famously used the press, and his great name (With perhaps the quiet blessings of his father, the shrewd Conrad Hilton?) and money, to bed folks like Elizabeth Taylor (who he married), Mamie Van Doren, Natalie Woods, and any other budding starlet the Hollywood studios set up for him so that they could possibly get publicity on the society pages for one of their new actresses.

In fact, it also can be argued that Hilton's decision early on, to relocate his growing corporation to Los Angeles, and not New York City, or the center of American commerce in the West, San Francisco, or stay in Texas—was what made him so successful

For example, Conrad Hilton quickly understood the value of publicity (we call it "branding" today). Additionally, he turned out to be a master of the grand event when he launched one of his hotels.

Based in a town like Los Angeles, with few real businesses, the astute Conrad he had to have noticed how effectively the Jewish moguls that ran the movie industry used these two simple ideas to their greatest advantage.

Strangely enough, Taraborrelli, who is a life-long native of Los Angeles, does not get into this in his book. It's almost as if the Jewish moguls didn't exist in Beverly Hills and Bel-Air when Conrad lived there. They are strangely absent in the book.

***

But there is much, much more to Randy's book. It is a wonderful lesson in the value of family, and having an optimistic personality; and more importantly, the power of a good, insightful idea and the ability to act on that idea.

Because of this, this is really Conrad Hilton's book.

The more I read about the man who launched the Hilton brand, and became one of the richest men in America, I was truly amazed at what he was able to accomplish, and the fact that his family still thrives today.

Witness his great-granddaughter, Paris, and all the Hilton hotels spread over the world.

***

This remarkable journey to undreamed of affluence and vast power, and deep connections that reached all the way to the White House, with Conrad becoming an occasional golfing partner with President Eisenhower, began in much more humble circumstances.

His father, August Halvorsen Hilton (Gus), an immigrant from Norway, started out as a small store owner in San Antonio, Texas. He soon had eight children. As each child came into the world, he would add another room to the then dilapidated structure they called home.

The family prospered, however, and in that part of Texas, where they had Gus's store, he was soon known as "Colonel Hilton."

But disaster soon struck. Writes Taraborrelli, "In 1907, the financial panic that came without warning hit the country and all but wiped out Gus Hilton's finances. Gathering his family about him, Gus spelled out the dire situation and asked for suggestions. Casting his eyes to the floor, nineteen-year old Conrad announced, "We should open a hotel. Let's take five or six of our ten rooms (of the house in which they lived) and make a hotel. This place needs a hotel."'

The idea was a smashing success and word soon spread all the way to Chicago. According to the brainy Conrad Hilton, the word was "if you have to break up your sales trip, break it at San Antonio and try to get a room at Hilton's. They serve the best meal in the West and they have a boy there who is crackerjack at making things comfortable for you."

This attention to the needs of his guests, and the hard work of his entire family, is the keystone to Conrad Hilton's great success. As he has pointed out, although he ran things, everyone chipped in, especially his mother who cooked all the meals: "Travelers got cleanliness, comfort and a good table for their $2.50 a day, even though we served three bountiful meals. I wouldn't take a million dollars for what those days taught me...and I'd give a million dollars for one of the suppers my mother served."

This started Hilton down the road to first national, then international success, with the Hilton name becoming one of the most recognized in the world.

But Conrad Hilton paid a high personal toll for this great success. Although he was a great host and loved parties and dancing, at which he excelled, he was also a very lonely man. His marriage to his first wife, Mary, produced three sons, but faltered.

His eventual marriage to the greedy, self-centered narcissist Zsa Zsa didn't last long, but it did produce a daughter, who Conrad always suspected wasn't his.

After that, he did not remarry again until he was eighty-eight years old. For three decades, the only women who stayed overnight in his huge mansion in Bel-Air were the help. He even would not let his daughter Francesca stay with him, when she once begged him that she had to get away from the ever-demanding Zsa Zsa.

***

There is much to learn from reading *The Hiltons*. As I hinted at the beginning of this review, all the gossip is here, but also a brilliant blueprint of how to put together such a large enterprise.

The Harvard Business School should recommend this book to their students. They could learn much about the reality of business.

Wilson

By A. Scott Berg

Reviewed by Fred Beauford

Woodrow Wilson

I was already predisposed to reviewing A. Scott Berg's latest biography,

this one on President Woodrow Wilson, entitled appropriately, *Wilson*, and

was not deterred by the hefty 743 pages.

When I was teaching the history of American Film at a number of universities, I made his book, *Goldwyn: A Biography*, required reading. I thought it was a well-written, deeply researched look at how early Hollywood developed.

Reading *Wilson*, which has Berg's considerable narrative skills in full display once again, I was drawn back to a subject that has always held the greatest interest for me for most of my adult life: the two narratives of American history (there is also a third one), one white, the other black.

One: "The Shining City on the Hill"; the other: "Behold, the Iceman cometh. Beware, destroyer of worlds."

And no one in American history best embodies both of these worlds better than Woodrow Wilson.

This is also the third book on American Presidents I have reviewed in the last two years (Andrew Johnson, Theodore Roosevelt and now Wilson).

What I can say about all three men, despite my personal aversion to much of their domestic policy's concerning blacks, with both Johnson and Wilson also having a deep seeded hated of black people—I have come away from reading these books with the realization that being President of the United States is one tough job, indeed.

The challenge quickly became clear to former political science professor Woodrow Wilson when his ideas were no longer theories to be discussed and debated in class, but could result in real lives lost.

Wilson, a progressive, wanted to focus his administration on domestic issues and curb the power of the wealthy and well connected. In this vein he had much success in his first year in passing progressive laws.

He also started what would be, after he was finished, the total segregation of Washington, thereby wiping out years of progress made by blacks in the civil service.

However, soon the rest of the world came knocking at the White House door. In his second year as president, in 1914, the Mexican dictator Victoriano Huerta would give Wilson his first real life lesson in what it means to be the commander-in-chief.

Writes Berg in a chapter entitled "Baptism, "…the Administration had learned that a ship had left Havana for Veracruz laden with 1,333 boxes of German guns intended for Huerta."

The strong man, General Huerta was under siege by the likes of General Francisco "Pancho" Villa and Emiliano Zapata, and the majority of the Mexican public.

The Senate had just given Wilson authority to employ the armed forces if needed against countries like Mexico "for unequivocal amends for affronts and indignities."

Wilson decided to use this new power to see that the guns did not fall into the hands of the hated despot, General Huerta.

On April 21, 1914, 800 Marines and Sailors landed at the Veracruz waterfront, and by the end of the next day they had overrun the town. Nineteen Americans died in the fighting, and seventy were wounded; more than a hundred Mexicans died.

Notes Berg, "He (Wilson) would later admit that he could not dismiss the thought of the young men killed in Mexico. "

"It was right to send them," President Wilson confided later to a friend, "but that does not mitigate the sorrow for their deaths—and *I* am responsible for their being there."

In a few short months, those 19 Americans and 100 Mexican dead would pale in significance, as on June 28, 1914 a teenaged Bosnian Serb shot Archduke Franz Ferdinand in Sarajevo, killing the heir apparent of the mighty Austro-Hungarian Empire, and sending the world into an orgy of violence it had never witnessed before.

As much as Wilson said that he wanted America to stay out of the wars in Europe, with the American public wanting no part of yet another European conflict, only this one bloodier than the American Civil War, which had set the gold standard for bloodshed—we ended up in the trenches in his second term, after he had won on the slogan, "He kept us out of war."

(Does this sound like most of our presidents, anyone, including Obama?)

***

The story of Wilson's rise to worldwide prominence is well presented in *Wilson,* warts and all. This is a wonderful book that I could barely put down, even as hefty as it was. A. Scott Berg is to be congratulated for yet another job well done.

1983: Reagan, Andropov, and a World on the Brink

By Taylor Downing

Da Capo Press | 2018 | 400 pages

Reviewed by Fred Beauford

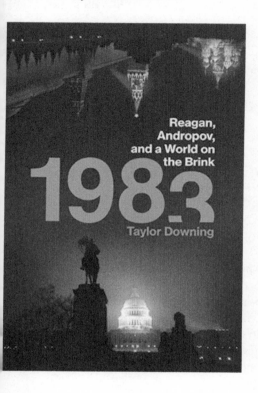

Scary Stuff

When I was just a teenager I can remember thinking that because I

lived in New York City, I was going to one day, perhaps soon, witness a

bright flash of light and be already dead before I got to hear the enormous

roar behind that blinding light. So far, years later, I still walk the streets of

New York City, and it is as intact and full of life, even more so, as it was

years ago.

However, author Taylor Downing book, *1983: Reagan, Andropov, and a*

World on the Brink, gave me the chills as he described how I, and millions

others, almost got fried.

This segment from his prologue says it all: "This [book] highlights…the

story of the 1983 war scare when the Soviets convinced themselves that

the United States was preparing to launch a nuclear first strike against

them… It shows how minor and unpredictable events can rapidly escalate

into major confrontations. And it climaxes with a night on which the Soviet

nuclear arsenal was put on to maximum alert, when missiles were

deployed to action stations… If these missiles had been fired it would have

prompted a nuclear exchange that would have destroyed much of North

America, most of Asia, probably all of Europe. The fallout would have

brought down a nuclear winter that would have covered Earth for years or decades to come. The death toll would have been counted in the hundreds of millions, dwarfing every conflict in human history"

How did this nightmare come about? Taylor Downing gives us a riveting account in this book, but first we have the two men who held the fate of the world in their hands: President Ronald Reagan of the United States of America and General Secretary of the Communist Party of the Soviet Union Yuri Andropov.

Reagan had recently turned 70, then the oldest man to run for president, and Andropov was 68, when General Secretary Leonid Brezhnev\ died on November 10, 1982, and he was chosen by a handful of elderly men who ran the Soviet Union. Andropov also, like with President Reagan, was the oldest man elected to hold his leadership position.

Most of world knew a great deal about President Reagan: radio, movie and television star; two-term governor of California, and finally, President of the United States. And he was one of the loudest voices against "godless Communism" and the "evil empire" of the Soviet Union.

By contrast, outside of Russia few knew anything about Andropov. Author Downing points out that "In the 1970s and 1980s, Western observers of events behind closed doors of the Politburo and the Central

Committee of the Communist Party of the Soviet Union were known as Kremlinologists."

These "experts" were taken aback when "a pale, stooping elderly man in heavy glasses stepped forward."

However, Andropov was as strong as Reagan's Americanism in his deeply held belief in Marxism/Leninism. He joined the Young Communist League at the age of sixteen. Then Joseph Stalin was the leader of the Soviet Union and Adolf Hitler was about to ravage Russia and most of Europe. Andropov rose quickly through the ranks, until in May 1967 he was appointed head of the famed, and deeply feared KGB, a huge organization with perhaps a half a million employees. It controlled spy missions both domestic and worldwide.

In that sense, it was wise for the master spymaster, to keep a low profile, which Andropov did until he was suddenly thrust into the world spotlight.

One of the problems that soon faced the aging rulers of Russia was Ronald Reagan. In fact, as I read this book, I felt that the author was clearly blaming Reagan for almost blowing up the world. The author writes, "The Soviet leadership was looking at a President who had spent much of his life mounting an anti-communist crusade and whose ideology was deeply opposed to theirs."

What scared them the most was first, Reagan's rearming. Writes Downing, "He planned for total defense spending from 1982 to 1989 to increase to $2.7 trillion. This amounted to the biggest peacetime build-up of military spending in American history."

Added to that was the placing in Europe of the Pershing 11 missile that could carry a nuke to the windows of the Kremlin in only six minutes. And to top it off, President Reagan proposed the Strategic Defense Initiative, quickly dubbed "Star Wars" by the press. The aim was to put in place ways to shoot down any missile coming from anywhere in the world. This idea included stationing lasers in space to kill the missiles before they reentered the earth.

At this point the Russian economy was a disaster. Food and general goods and services were a joke. There was no way that the old men in the Kremlin could compete with America and Reagan knew it, and the old men knew it.

Andropov and his close associates also came to the belief that what Reagan was really up to was a first strike against them. He had already said publicly that he thought that Mutual Assured Destruction (MAD) was "crazy." The Pershing 11, which was introduced in Europe to counter the Soviet's SS 22, really kept them up at night. They were under the opinion that it was a first strike weapon, which confirmed their belief that Reagan wanted to "decapsulate" the leadership of the Soviet Union. They became so obsessed with the idea that they started Operation RYaN, a human intelligence operation to keep a sharp eye on any movement in the West that would indicate that the USA was about to launch a first strike against them.

This all came to a head in November 1983 with a war game by NATO titled Able Archer 83. By this time, Andropov was very ill and was being treated at the Kuntsevo Clinic twenty miles out of Moscow. And, like Reagan, he had nearby the "football," a briefcase that contained the codes need to launch nuclear weapons.

As the war game became more alarming, "At his bedroom in the Kuntsevo Clinic, a military aide sat beside Andropov with the *chegget* ("football") ready to send out the nuclear launch codes. Marshal Ogarkov, one of the men authorized to launch nuclear weapons, settled into the central command bunker outside of Moscow for the night."

The KGB and the GRU was sending out "Super Urgent Flash" telegrams to "their people around the world that the situation was now critical, and that the NATO exercise was in all likelihood preparation for sudden nuclear attack."

Their double agent West Germany Rainer Rupp, who had penetrated the upper level of NATO headquarters, was asked to keep his eyes open.

Writes Downing, "Rupp could see that there was absolutely no gearing up for war at NATO headquarters. The war game was just that." And he was able to send this important message back in time to the leadership in the Kremlin.

Notes Downing, "A paranoid leadership could never trust one source that stood out against the rest. But almost certainly Rainer Rupp played a small part in helping to save the world from a nuclear holocaust."

The old men in the Kremlin finally stood down, along with all their missiles, submarines, and aircraft all loaded and ready to launch.

So, we can now see that Reagan and his associates had no idea that Andropov and his associates were so frightened by Reagan. And Reagan later confided to an associate that he "shuddered" when he found out that his words and taunts almost ended human life on this planet.

President Trump, and every president from this moment on should read this book.

Burning Bridges: America's 20-Year Crusade to Deport Labor Leader Harry Bridges

Peter Afrasiabi

Reviewed by Fred Beauford

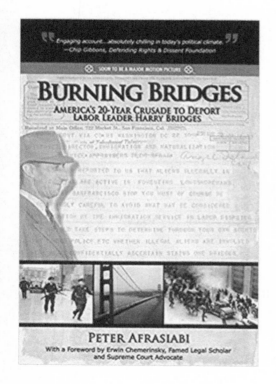

An Amazing Story

When I moved to San Francisco in 1980, I was struck by how most blacks lived in the large Victorian houses that the city was so famous for. I also soon discovered that in the Bay Area, from as far away as Vallejo, to Richmond, Berkeley and Oakland, there were large communities of blacks living in nice, large single-family homes.

"You can thank Harry Bridges for that," one of my colleagues at my department at UC Berkeley informed me. He also said dryly that those "days were numbered because most of those houses were now owned by elderly black women. The gays and the Chinese are going to get them soon."

I knew little about Harry Bridges at that time. I knew that he was the leading labor leader on the West Coast, and he ran the longshoreman's union. But that was about it. But there was a hell of a lot I didn't know, and this book provided me with a hallowing tale that was well worth knowing about: the 20-year crusade to deport Harry Bridges. But what made so many in the United States so fearful of Bridges?

Bridges was born in Melbourne, Australia, on July 28,1901. He arrived in the United States as a teenage sailor in 1920. By the tumultuous '30s, he was working in San Francisco as a longshoreman. He was also knee deep in union politics and soon became an outspoken, daring and popular labor leader, organizing longshoremen on the entire West Coast. Afrasiabi points out that "Bridges tolerated no racial discrimination in the union," something few labor leaders did in the '30s.

All of this soon put a huge bullseye on Bridges' back. Writes Afrasiabi, "at the same time, various quarters had started to take note of Bridges and his perceived agitation. Government agents working for the National Rifle Association had sent messages to Washington, D.C., warning that Bridges was communistic in nature and would lead to communist control of the waterfront."

Other union leaders, jealous of his growing power and influence among the working class and shipowners, who did not want to pay the living wages that Bridges demanded, joined in on the attacks. But Bridges organized longshoremen all the way to Washington so owners could no longer just move their ships to another port.

Notes Afrasiabi, "These communiques to the halls of power—all revolving around fears of communism on the waterfront, and specifically about Bridges as an alleged centerpiece of the communist movement— started as a slow trickle in 1933, but events were about to turn into a raging river."

By the mid-'30s an axis of private organizations and government agencies, mainly The American Legion, and the House Un-American Activities Committee (HUAC) were determined to prove that Harry Bridges was indeed a card-carrying member of the Communist Party and should be sent back to Australia.

The government and his other distractors had a powerful weapon to use against Bridges, who always maintained that he was not a member of the Communist Party, because "under American immigration law of the time, if a non-citizen was affiliated with an organization that advocated the overthrow of the government, then he could be deported. The Communist Party was one of the primary organizations that triggered governmental deportation actions. Thus, if Bridges could be proven a member of the party, then he could be deported and his radical voice for labor permanently silenced," writes Afrasiabi.

The bulk *of Burning Bridges* deals with the many trails, hearings and even a short stay in jail for Bridges. But despite the machinations of his opponents—and it was a series of hair-raising events, of lies so unbelievable, that trial after trial, for 20 years, starting in 1934 and ending, finally in 1955—each verdict was overturned. They could never pin the charge on Harry Bridges that he was a member of the Communist Party, and he was never deported.

In the end, this was great news for the men he championed, who endured the backbreaking work of loading and unloading shipping from around the world. They did finally become well compensated for their work, including the work of black Americans. And, it wasn't the ship owners or political witch-hunts that spelled the end for these men, but in 1962, the Port of Oakland began to admit container ships, and the need for thousands of men with strong backs was soon all over.

This was why my colleague at UC Berkeley said dryly that for those blacks, still living large in great houses, their "days were numbered."

Americana

Ella: A Biography

By Geoffrey Mark

Reviewed by Fred Beauford

I fell in love with Ella Fitzgerald in 1980. I had listened to her for years on television, on the radio and in the occasional movie that featured her. Of course, she was a great singer, but she often seemed to me old fashioned. For example, her breakout hit, which occurred when she was a still teenager, and I was not yet born, was in 1938, "A Tisket, a Tasket."

I had never owned any of her records despite my being the editor of *Black Creation: The Quarterly of Black Arts and Letters, Soul*, the magazine of black music, and *Neworld: The Multi-Cultural Magazine of the Arts.*

However, that changed when I received two CD sets from a record company that wanted me to review them in Neworld Magazine. They were *The George and Ira Gershwin Songbook*, and *The Cole Porter Songbook*. In a few shorts months after receiving them, hating LA so much that I turned and gave it the finger as I rode the Greyhound bus out of town, I packed up everything I owned, including the unopened CD's, closed my beloved magazine down, and moved from Los Angeles to San Francisco.

However, I was still teaching a Magazine Making and Publishing course at USC, one night a week, the first such magazine course of its kind on the West Coast. I would take the Greyhound in the morning and take the redeye bus at night, right after my class was over.

To deal with the tedium of sitting on a bus for so many hours, for some reason, I first brought along the Gershwin songbook, plugged in my earphones, and soon fell deeply in love with such a marvelous voice.

Now I knew why *Downbeat,* the renowned jazz magazine, year after year, named her the number one jazz singer in the world.

***

Ella, like many black singers born at the time (1918 in Newport News, Virginia) was the product of a broken home of common-law parents.

Her mother Tempie and her father William, soon separated and Tempie moved the family to Yonkers, in Westchester County, New York. Mother and daughter moved in with Tempie's Portuguese lover, Joseph Da Silva, often referred to as Ella's stepfather. Ella always said nice things about him to the press, but author Geoffrey Mark uncovers the sex abuse that he inflicted on her when she was a child.

They lived in an ethnically mixed area of Italians, Spanish and blacks. Her mother died at the age of 38. The reason for her early death is murky, and afterwards things became rough for the young Ella.

Writes Mark, "Ella's aspirations for Yonkers success were ended when her hardworking mother died in 1932. The next two years were perhaps Ella's most difficult. Da Silva turned increasingly to alcohol and increasingly turned his attention to young Ella. Whether he was simply comforting himself from grief, taking out his anger and grief on the youngster, or actually saw her as a sex object, the man was sexually abusing her."

Two years later Ella left his house and moved in with her mother's sister at 145th Street in Harlem. That didn't work out well, and she tried to run away. She was caught by the authorities and sent to the New York State Training School for Girls.

Writes Mark, "It boggles the mind that this Dickensian institution had Ella Fitzgerald in their midst but would not allow her to sing in the choir. It was restricted to white girls only."

She was asked to come back after she became famous, but "turned them down in colorful language."

She finally fled from the Institution and became semi-homeless on the streets of Harlem, sleeping where ever she could, hanging out with "Ladies of the Night" and becoming a number runner at the height of the Great Depression. But she found out that she could sing.

As almost always for blacks, it started in the church, in this case the Bethany African Methodist Episcopal Church of Harlem.

At this time black Harlem had three major assets: music, dance and singing. One white wag even noted, "The Negro is in trouble again, and yet again, trying to sing his way out of it."

Well, Ella did manage to sing her way out of harm's way big time. Writes Mark, "The Apollo Theatre had a policy of having an amateur night, a performance of new talent after the 'real' show was over. The concept of having these showcases began at Harlem's Lafayette Theatre on 132nd in 1933. The winner received a prize of a trophy, cash, or perhaps a professional booking."

In January 1934, Ella's life changed forever. She got her shot at the Apollo amateur night and sang a song named, "Judy." When she finished, the often-unruly crowd quieted, and "you could hear a rat piss on cotton," someone wrote.

She then sang "Believe It Beloved."

Said Mark, "Ella brought the house down, winning first prize, and a reportedly $25.00. Had she not won the contest, Ella would have never pursued a career as a vocalist. She called the evening, 'the turning point of my life. Once up there, I felt the acceptance and love from the audience—I knew I wanted to sing before people the rest of my life.'"

And she did just that with successes almost unparalleled in American history. She died on June 18, 1996, at age 78, just a few years after her last performance.

Her contemporary, Billie Holiday (Lady Day) and later, Tina Turner, both got their day on the big screen. Giving what I now know about Ella Fitzgerald, she should also be given the honor of the big screen. After such a harrowing childhood, she rose to be the leading lady of American song. How many Americans can say that! This is America at its finest.

This book will give you a great tour of Ella's musical career, along with passing glances of her private life. It is well worth purchasing.

Twain's Feast: Searching for America's Lost Food in the Footsteps of Samuel Clemens
by Andrew Bears

Reviewed by Fred Beauford

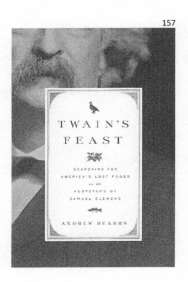

When I was the editor of the *Crisis* magazine, during the first years of the '90s, I embarked on several press junkets organized and paid for by the giant oil company, Chevron, which had its headquarters in San Francisco.

They had assembled a small group of magazine editors from around the country. We all—black, white and Hispanic, male and female—all edited publications that were thought to influence public policy; so, without anyone saying it, it was obvious to all of us what the point of these trips really was really.

The first year we were first taken to Alaska, where we stayed in Anchorage, and piled daily into two large helicopters to journey northward to Prince William Sound, where the worst oil spill in American history had recently occurred.

***

Journalists can sometimes be a deeply cynical, mistrustful group of folks. While standing on the banks of one of the many islands in the Sound, I stuck a toe in the cold Artic Ocean (just so I could claim that this was third ocean in which I had done so), as Chevron explained how things had returned to close to normal.

All at once, a large fish breached the water. Just as quickly, a huge bald eagle swooped down from one of the tall trees that surrounded the Sound, grabbed the fish between its sharp talons, and flew off.

I exclaimed to the editor next to me, in total wonderment and awe, perhaps from watching so many animal shows on PBS, "Holy Shit! Did you see that?"

"Chevron probably staged it," he coolly replied, unimpressed.

***

The following year we were treated to the French Quarter in New Orleans, and several more helicopter trips, only this time to off-shore oil rigs, far out in the Gulf of Mexico.

All of these memories come pouring back as I continue to witness, like most Americans, the sickening sight of vast amounts of oil pouring into the Gulf; back then, one of the top executives from Chevron assured us (editors), with great confidence, (as we had lunch on one of the rigs in a pristine lunch room, surrounded by pervasive signs warning against any kind of spark or flame), that such a thing could never happen.

And, strangely enough, reading Andrew Beahrs' *Twain's Feast: Searching For America's Lost Foods in the Footsteps of Samuel Clemens*, also brought those trips back to me.

Like Clemens, as a young man I was a wanderer and note-taker, who marveled over and over again about the different experiences I had encountered nationwide. And what could be a more different than the northern tip of the New World, and the southern tip of mainland America?

Yet, from the point of view of experiencing local cuisine, Alaska proved to be disappointing. Anchorage was filled with Pizza Huts, MacDonalds, Burger Kings and Wendys. For a moment I thought I was back in downtown Burbank. I came all the way up here for a Big Mac? Where was my reindeer stew?

***

But fortunately, New Orleans the next year lived up to its billing. I felt that the people there went out of their way to present authentic local food and superb preparation. I discovered that the Gulf of Mexico was a chef's and eater's delight, and that the many world-class creative chefs and restaurateurs in New Orleans seemed to take great pleasure in showing off their culinary expertise.

***

America was once filled with distinct local cuisine that could perhaps rival the Gulf. Beahrs points out that the slow erosion and disappearance of distinct local food started long before the franchising of America.

For the much-prized prairie chicken it was replaced with corn, "When it comes to the prairies," he writes, "the effect of America's subsidizing of industrial corn has been nuclear, reducing thousands of species to one, or at best a handful."

In the case of the tasty Lake Tahoe Lahontan cutthroat trout that Twain loved so much, dams, miners, loggers and the Army Corp of Engineers soon led to its demise.

In addition to the usual suspects, there was also the impact of railroads and steamships, "which carried ice to cool rooms, frost drinks—and, of course, to preserve and ship food. In 1842 railroads were experimenting with using ice-filled cars to ship fish. Exactly twenty-five years later, one J.B. Sutherland received a patent for a refrigerated train car," Beahrs writes.

With Sutherland's patent, the Big Macs slowly began their century long journey to complete domination.

***

One common theme in Twain's writing regarding a meal, was his longing for food cooked in the "Southern style."

Beahrs writes: "Twain lived in New York and New England for as long as he did the South. Still, he remained nearly nationalistic about Southern Cooking. Like most of his contemporaries, Twain probably didn't think much about the dishes' origins…he didn't name the enslaved women who worked in the log kitchen…or the smokehouse behind that."

"Though these women were almost certainly several generations removed from Africa, their skills—and those of millions of women like them—were anchored in the cooking and customs of their great grandmothers' homeland…West Africans shared six major cooking techniques: boiling in water, steaming in leaves, frying in deep oil, toasting beside the fire, roasting over the fire, and baking in ashes."

The black slaves on the young Samuel Clemens' uncle's farm employed all of these cooking techniques. The now famous Mark Twain spent the rest of his adult life savoring the memories of this great, well-prepared feast that he knew as a child.

Beahrs' has the acute insight of both the historian and the feature writer and *Twain's Feast* is filled with well-drawn portraits, complete with recipes, as Mark Twain traveled far and wide, with memories of the antebellum South always a part of him. He also points out how much we have lost in our headlong rush for convenience, speed and "progress."

My one regret about *Twain's Feast* is that the book could have used some closer editing. Many of Andrew Beahrs' chapters go on far too long, and lose their storytelling power. This book could have easily been cut down by at least 10 percent.

With that caveat in mind, this is an American history book that will no doubt *not* be used in history courses, where it should be taught. I hope not, as that would be a loss. This is American history at its best and fullest.

In the Basement of the Ivory Tower: Confessions of an Accidental Academic
By Professor X

A tale of two accidental professors

Reviewed by Fred Beauford

This is an essay about two "accidental academics" with two very different

experiences in such a role. Although I once shared many of the problems Professor X

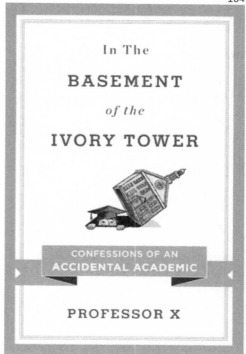

writes about in his first book, including standing in front of many college students who hated the written word, I didn't start in the basement of academia as he, but far upstairs, in the elevated tower of academe.

In 1975, I started teaching in the Department of Journalism at the University of Southern California (USC), a school then best known internationally for its rich kids, running backs and a first-rate film school.

Following that tenure, I became a Visiting Professor at UC Berkeley, then ranked, in the four years I taught there, as the number two highest ranking university in the nation, after Harvard.

I don't say all of this to brag, or hold my nose up at Professor X, who has only taught at community colleges; but because similarly, my first full time teaching position was as an Associate professor at an open enrollment college on Long Island. This is where Professor X's past and present, and mine, collide, and what made his book resound so resolutely with me.

Here is how Professor X ended up as "a lowly adjunct" at several community colleges: "My wife and I marked the turn of the millennium by buying a home that we really couldn't afford....Not long after we closed on the house, we both realized that one of us would have to work a second job in order to maintain a middle-class existence. I am the proud possessor of the most useless advanced degree there is—a Master of Fine Arts in Creative Writing, which qualifies me to do very little other than teach introductory-level college courses. And so I awoke one morning from uneasy dreams and found myself transformed into a part-time instructor of college English."

On the other hand, my elite status came not because of race, or even an advanced degree. I merely had a lowly B.S. from NYU, but what I also had was the fact that I was one the few magazine Editor-in-Chief/Publishers on the West Coast, and my magazine, Neworld: The Multi-Cultural Magazine of the Arts, was kicking serious butt in Los Angeles.

I had put together a course on magazine publishing, and started shopping it around; leaning boldly forward, telling chair after chair who granted me an interview, that I was a cowboy, willing to fail right in front a bunch of students, because what I was teaching them was something I was living with daily.

As I later told my students at USC, at the start of each semester, "I could go out of business right before your eyes, before this semester is over, if some of things I am going to tell you don't quite work out as I thought."

What could be a more compelling, dramatic way to open a course?

The community colleges all said I needed at least a master's degree in order to teach. But USC was something altogether different. Dr. Barrows, a friendly, middle-aged white man, who I later learned was eager to get back into real journalism, and who was to become my chair, was becoming increasingly delighted as I outlined the course I had in mind; and he looked almost as if he was thinking, "How did I get so lucky?"

His yes was the fastest yes in my life. My chair was not even warm.

In a few months, the journalism department introduced the first "Magazine Making and Publishing" course on the West Coast; which I taught for six years before I left for UC Berkeley.

And, as I had thought, my narrative was indeed compelling, as each year my class grew larger, After the first semester, the department had a guard checking ID, posted outside of my classroom door for at least three weeks into the semester, to keep "ghosts" (non USC students) from slipping in after I told the journalism department I had 24 students, when only 21 were registered.

One ghost drove up all the way from San Diego. That smart, intense young man, who had asked such great, probing questions in my introductory class, and two others, were soon caught, and thrown, without protest, into the streets.

***

But what of Professor X, at his community college? What was his first time on the same job like?

After a bravura opening performance, Professor X saw clearly that he was able to elicit genuine excitement in the students who sat before him. That intoxicating feeling didn't last long, however, as he soon became appalled at what he discovered about his students after his first written assignment.

"I put down my mug of coffee," Professor X noted, "I looked over, for the third and perhaps the fourth time, my stack of baseline essays. I did not then own a cell phone and had never sent or received a text message, but I needed the phrase that would become one of the greatest of electronic clichés.

"WTF. What The Fuck.

"The essays were terrible, but the word 'terrible' doesn't begin to convey the state these things were in. My God. Out of about fifteen students, at least ten seemed to have no familiarity with the English language."

***

At both USC and UC Berkeley, one always had to be on one's toes, which made teaching such a great delight, because you learned from the students, as they learned from you; and the class discussion after my formal, 45-minute lecture, was where the true learning began.

"But Professor Beauford, wasn't it 1915 when the Supreme Court declared the Edison Trust illegal, not 1914?' I almost expected a duh to accompany that statement.

"Yes, yes, quite right, Amy. My mistake. You can leave now, you have an automatic A."

I loved the intellectual gun slinging one expected when teaching at an elite school, where everyone in my class thought they were smarter than me (at USC my students didn't necessarily think that they were smarter, but they all knew with absolute certainty that they were far richer, and far more connected than I would ever be. They didn't call USC, the University of Serious Connections for nothing.

But there were few gunslingers on Long Island, and precious fewer at the community colleges Professor X taught at.

***

What's was even more disheartening for Professor X was the fact that although a whopping 73 percent of college students are taught by adjuncts or graduate students, "...we are nothing less than academic hit men. We are paid by the college to perform the dirty work that no one else wants to do, the wrenching, draining, sorrowful business of teaching and failing the unprepared."

Adjuncts have no benefits, have no influence in the departments in which they teach, and make on average, what they could have made working part time at Macy's. As a Visiting Professor as UC Berkeley, I was paid half of what a full professor was paid, for teaching one course, three hours a week; while the adjuncts in my department, working the same hours, were paid a miserly $ 2,000 a semester.

***

I can also see that I had several advantages over Professor X., while teaching the same kind of students he had encountered. I soon saw clearly that I was no longer among the intellectual elite here on Long Island. I realized quickly just how anti-text so many of the students were, and I was on the verge of leaving, or having a nervous breakdown.

I then discovered that the college had an awesome AV (Audio and Video) department. What's more, they also had an amazing, spanking new, state of the arts television studio, which so far had rarely been used.

I was a journalist, still the editor of *The Crisis*, a magazine published by the national NAACP, and founded by W.E.B. Du Bois in 1910. There were photographs of people with mutton chops on my walls in my office on Fifth Avenue.

I had been recruited for this position, and had not sought it out; I was an accidental academic.

However, from so many years of teaching The History of the Mass Media, and being heavily influenced by one of the best minds of the 20th Century, the great media thinker Marshall McLuhan, and although I had always worked in print, I saw text as just another information medium, especially after coming to realize that the electronic revolution Samuel Morse unleashed in 1844 had now gained an unchallenged hegemony on the dissemination of information, far surpassing the world changing print revolution Johannes Gutenberg ushered in in 1440.

The non-reading students were obviously more the beneficiaries of Morse's revolution than the others, where text still mattered. The spoken word, and what they saw on television, or heard on the radio, or on recordings, vigorously competed with text, and nothing could change that.

Because of this insight, which perhaps came about because journalists (and good novelists) can be oddly detached when all hell is breaking lose, the fly on the wall, as I have been sometimes called; and because teaching history provides many compelling lessons, I hadn't yet dismissed the many students who hated print with a passion I often found deeply compelling.

In the AV department at my little college there was a treasure trove of classic documentaries, old television shows, political debates, famous radio shows, classic blues and jazz, and my personal favorite, Doo-Wop, and so much more of world and American history,

And the television studio was just sitting there, waiting to be used.

If I could only pull it all together, then I could reach everyone in my classes, including the non-readers. It didn't take long for my multi-media approach to teaching to cause a remarkable turnaround in my students.

What delighted me most was when we were in the television studio, as I taught them how to put together news and talk shows. Year after year, the students who once sat quietly, meekly, in the back of the room during the print segment, took over and elbowed everyone else aside.

I was once more having fun teaching.

Professor X's book, In the Basement of the *Tower: Confessions* Ivory *of an Accidental Academic*, took me back in time to that success, because I have often wondered, if I had been teaching the same kind of classes he taught, even with all the wonderful AV resources my college on Long Island had provided me, would such a multi-media approach produce the same amazing results?

Always Plenty to Do: Growing up on a Farm in the Long Ago
by Pamela Riney-Kehrberg

Reviewed by Fred Beauford

Although this slim volume is for young readers, I was drawn to it for many reasons, one of which was because I had personally lived some of what Professor Pamela Riney-Kehrberg describes in her book (You can find my account at *Neworld Review*, No. 5, Chapter One of my memoir, *And Mistakes Made Along the Way* "The Morton's of Virginia"). I was familiar first hand with slopping

the hogs, outhouses, pulling weeds, milking cows, drawing water from the well, wringing the head off a chicken, chopping wood, and gathering whatever food we could through fishing, hunting and poaching, if the case called for it. We had great food, took baths Saturday nights in a big round tin tub in the kitchen next to a large, wood burning stove, and were surrounded day and night by a small army of brothers, cousins, uncles and aunts, as well as closeted white relatives we only whispered about.

Her book had me pondering about our brave new world of machines that now do the chores that we once did, and I recalled a quote from a historian that said, "The Agrarian Age was the most grim, brutish, barbaric period in human history," and wondered how in the future, a similar historian would characterize our plugged-in world of the early 21st Century.

In *Always Plenty to Do,* there is little wonder there was plenty to do, because this was a world of ceaseless labor, with only a 50/50 chance that locusts, drought, or more rain that one needed, would render one's efforts meaningless. This is what most humans experienced before the age of machines, and profound, life-changing innovations like electricity.

In this world, young people, as Professor Riney-Kehrberg points out, almost as soon as they were able to walk, played just as important a role in the survival of the family as anyone.

"If you stepped back in time and visited a farm in 1900," she writes, "you would see a very different world from the one you live in. The food didn't come from a box or a can but from the garden or the henhouse. Most of the clothes people wore were home-made too, and the houses were small and cramped. All around you, boys, girls, mothers, and fathers worked, doing the day's chores and making their home a good place to live."

Schooling for young people often meant a one-room schoolhouse, which just as often would "require a two-mile hike across fields, through the woods, and over a stream.... Farm children worked outside in every kind of weather, from the blazing hot summer sun to the freezing cold winter wind. The children worked more than they played or studied, and they often sacrificed time from school and play to tend to the needs of their parents' farms," she writes.

Professor Riney-Kehrberg indicated that this time lasted to the end of World War I. By this time, we started seeing the slow impact of the world of machines coming into play: tractors, combines, school buses, electricity, indoor plumbing and central heating. However, this march of progress took considerable time to spread to the world that we know today.

For example, my grandfather's large farm in Northern Virginia, at the time I lived there in the late '40s, was still a place of horse-drawn transportation, outhouses, large cast-iron stoves that relied on wood; and all of us on the farm were very aware of the fact that we created most of what we consumed by our efforts, including those of a small tot like me.

But we did have electricity!

One final personal note about life on the farm for a young person, not even in the second grade: I often chuckle to myself when I hear people talking about how we must shelter young minds from being exposed to sex at too early an age. What a laugh! On the farm, the whole damn thing was about sex. Without sex, the more the better, there wouldn't be a farm, or food to eat, or clothes to wear.

Chickens were screwing chickens, pigs were screwing pigs, cows were screwing cows, goats were screwing goats and Grandpa and Grandma were busy producing 14 children!

Just walking out of our big white house in the morning was like walking into one big porno movie.

If you didn't know about the birds and bees, and where babies came from by the time you were five, you were a dullard indeed, and hadn't yet opened your eyes.

Professor Riney-Kehrberg has produced an insightful book for young people to give them some idea of what life on the farm was really like, and help ground them in early Americana. And for the more thoughtful of young readers of her book a deep insight into why slavery existed for so long, and why so many young farm boys everywhere in the world eagerly volunteered to join whatever army offered them escape, despite the many dangers, and why so many fled that harsh life as soon as they could, and why cities held such allure.

The Whip
by Karen Kondazian

Reviewed by Fred Beauford

One thing I really like about this job is that I get to discover promising new talent far outside of the world of agents, New York publishers, academics, and establishment book reviewers.

Karen Kondazian's debut novel, *The Whip*, is in that category. Her well-written book, based on a true story, displays all the confidence of a seasoned novelist. I didn't detect one false note.

The Whip was inspired by the true story of a woman, Charlotte "Charley" Parkhurst (1812-1879), who lived most of her extraordinary life as a man in the Old West.

As a young woman in Rhode Island, she fell in love with a runaway slave and had his child, which brought about unforgivable human cruelty.

The destruction of Charlotte's family is detailed with horrendous details.

She then journeyed to California, dressed as a man, to track the person who instigated the slaughter of her family, someone from the orphanage, s who she once considered almost a brother

Charley became a renowned stagecoach driver for Wells Fargo (a whip). She killed a famous outlaw, had a secret love affair, and lived with a housekeeper who, unaware of her true sex, fell in love with her.

Charley was the first woman to vote in America in 1868 (as a man).

This true story gives first-time author Kondazian, an actress with over 50 television and film credits, much to work with.

Charley's story begins in Boston in 1812, when, as a newborn, she is placed on the steps of an orphanage. Her mother gives a hearty knock on the door and then quickly flees.

Charlotte's "Charley" adventure has just begun, and what a great adventure it turned out to be. Charlotte often found herself at odds with the powers at The Home (the orphanage), comforted only, from early childhood, by another orphan, years older than she, Lee Colton, who would eventually become her hated nemesis.

Because of her willfulness, she was assigned to live and work in the stalls with the horses, managed by an older black man named Jonas. He treats her with kindness, and imparts much wisdom to her, becoming the closest thing she has had to a father.

Most importantly, he taught her how to deal with horses.

She takes his last name, Parkhurst, after he dies.

***

Anyone who has lived in the West will recognize the DNA traces of the fact that it was "Go West, young man," not young woman.

When Charlotte first arrived in Sacramento in 1849 disguised as a man, "she was taken aback by the dozens of barks, brigs, and schooners along the docks. They created a forest of masts…their cables looped around tree trunks and roots. The street was choked with stagecoaches and wagons, disgorging passengers, the passengers running for the boats. Men of every shape, color, and constitution were there—swearing, spitting, sweating, and shoving.

"Later, Charley would learn their names: Mexicans, Indians, Chinese, Basques, Croats. She noticed that there were no women of any shape or color."

Author Kondazian got it right, because in 1849, the year Charley landed in Northern California after a harrowing, four-month journey over land and sea, there were only 49 women in the entire city of San Francisco out of a population of 48,000.

This fact, often published in local newspapers, became a running joke among my friends in San Francisco who knew the history of this city in which we lived.

It's easy to see why this beautiful jewel of a city by The Bay went on to become the gay capital of America, if not the world.

***

The fighting over the few available women for the Euro-American settlers still resonates loudly out West to this very day.

***

I have often been accused of never meeting a book I didn't like. But try *The Whip* on, nevertheless, despite me. I think you will get as caught up in it as I was. This is classic Americana.

So Many Angels: A Family Crisis and the Community That Got Us Through It

By Diana Stelfox Cook

Reviewed by Fred Beauford

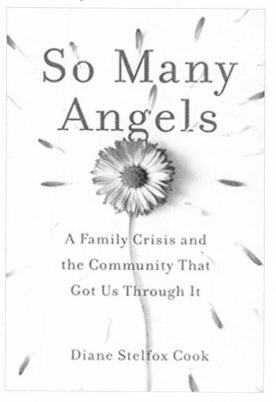

This Was No Big Apple

All it took was a single phone call, and Diana Cook's seemingly perfect marriage was over. Her husband, a grade schoolteacher and hockey coach, called to say that he was in jail for attempted solicitation of a fourteen-year-old boy over the internet.

All at once all hell breaks loose. What to tell her two young boys? What will her friends say? Will he lose his job? Will he go to jail? How could he do something like that?

But the worse was soon to come. After picking up her sons and telling them that "Boys, Dad and I had a big fight, and he's not going to come home tonight," the phone rings.

"We had been home an hour when the ringing phone startled me. I saw the *Boston Globe* on the caller ID screen, and I was stunned. I picked up the phone, and said "Hello," and a reporter barked at me, "Would you like to comment on your husband's arrest?"

A few minutes later the phone rang again, only this time it was from a reporter from a local television station.

Now it was time to call for help. First, it was Marylee. Then her friend Patty showed up "at seven in the morning with the local paper in her hand. Jed (the husband) was on the cover." Soon her house "was full of friends who had brought food and stopped by to see what they could do."

One of the things they tried to get Diane not to see, as she sat on her couch crying: Don't look out the window! "I ignored them," she wrote. "I felt compelled to look. I was shocked and totally unprepared for what I saw: every local media outlet had sent a truck… There were more than a dozen giant news vans parked on both sides of my usually quiet suburban street."

I was immediately drawn into this often-sad tale, and not just because of the graceful writing in this memoir and first book.

I am a New Yorker. The Big Apple. Something like what happened to her, and the uproar that it caused in my neck of the woods would have been buried in a paragraph on page 20 the next day, if at all, unless the perpetrator was a well-known celebrity. Then the tabloids would have a field day.

Cook had many problems to overcome, but was able to put her new life in order. But just when things had settled down and she was working full time, and caring for her two young boys, she was diagnosed with multiple sclerosis. Still, through it all she learned that even in her darkest moments she was not alone. Her community was there to help her and the boys. This is a book well worth reading, especially for us big city types. We have a lot to learn from it.

Plutocracy in America: How Increasing Inequality Destroys the Middle Class and Exploits the Poor

By Ronald P. Formisano

Reviewed by Fred Beauford

Plutocracy or Aristocracy?

The more I read this book, the more I felt that the real story was not that we have become a plutocracy (rule by the wealthy) but we are rapidly becoming an aristocracy (rule by a privileged class.)

Professor Ronald P. Formisano, who is the William T. Bryan Chair of American History at the University of Kentucky, informs us that the world I was born into, "from World War II to the late 1960s the benefits of a growing U.S. economy percolated from the bottom through the middle to the top of society. For three decades after 1945 a relatively equally distributed prosperity built a strong middle class that was the envy of the world. As John F. Kennedy put it, 'a rising tide lifts all boats.' Those in the lower classes gained as much or more than those in the higher ones.

"The current state of disequilibrium in the United States began in the 1970s, when the top 1 percent earned about 10 percent of the national income. Since then the income of the richest soared to 15-19 percent of the total in the late 1990s; in 2007, the richest 1 percent took home 23.5 percent of all income. In the upper precincts of the 0.1 percent, 13,000 households took in more than 11 percent of the nation's income."

It couldn't get any clearer than that. But what happened? How did this come about?

Plutocracy in America takes us down a path well trodden, covering the many whys—from government deregulation, a country flooded with cheap labor, both legal and illegal, and "technology and a virtual global media have led to rapid gains at the very top for the 'superstars' in business and elsewhere. Celebrities such as musicians, athletes, and movie stars now can reach millions of people worldwide and thus command enormous paychecks."

An example I often cite is the fact that Michael Jordan made $80 to $100 million dollars last year. He also made the same $80 million the year before that and the year before that. In fact, I doubt that Jordan can even remember the last time he made less that $80 million a year. And he is only in his early 50s!

This is what the good professor is talking about!

The book also takes us down a road few have dared to go. Professor Formisano cites a study by Enrico Moretti:

"Moretti's analysis affirms that the causes and consequences of inequality are multiple and interrelated. Some are unintended results of social progress, such as the phenomenon known as 'assortative mating.' As more women have acquired higher education, broken glass ceilings, and entered better-paying professions, they tended to marry other higher-income professionals, contributing to income inequality."

Here is my personal favorite example to illustrate the beast that we men are and why that very beastliness has always played a major role in the redistribution of wealth: Anna Nicole Smith was a high school dropout with a worthless husband and a child to support. One day she was pole dancing at Gigi's, a Houston strip joint, when an elderly man by the name of J. Howard Marshall rolled into her show in his custom-made wheel chair. Soon, he was at Gigi's on a regular basis, throwing more expenses gifts at Anna Nicole Smith than she knew existed in the many heavens folks love bragging about.

But he could afford it. He was worth 1.6 billion dollars. Three years later, the 26-year-old Smith and the 81-year-old Marshall married.

Marshall died a year later, no doubt with a smile on his wrinkled old face, and he left her a large fortune as a thank you for making the end of his life filled with such pleasure.

Now, I ask you, do you think that Martha Stewart, Oprah Winfrey, or any of those other overpaid, chattering women on television would do something like that!

Of course not. Mother Nature won't allow this to happen, not on her watch! So, for now, it's either you show up with a paycheck larger than theirs, or, forget about it, Bud.

It seems that until women can become as silly as men and stop hoarding their money, there's little hope for us.

Plutocracy in America is an interesting book. I am glad I read it.

Fear Be Thy Name

The Israel Lobby and U.S. Foreign Policy
By John J. Mearsheimer and Stephen M. Walt
Reviewed by Fred Beauford

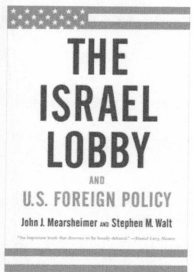

I witnessed first hand the tremendous power of the Jewish lobby in this country as a journalist in the '80s. I watched as a marginal Louis Farrakhan was almost instantly elevated as one of the most important leaders in the black community, even though, outside of his home base in Chicago, he wasn't even on the

189

radar screen of most Americans, even black Americans.

The truth, as we saw it, was that Farrakhan was just the leader of the Nation of Islam, a small religious sect that had its heyday under the leadership of the charismatic Malcolm X, but now enjoyed little support in black communities nationwide.

Yet, soon after Farrakhan started making critical remarks, aimed directly at Jews, he was in all the magazines, on the front page of newspapers, on the nightly television newscasts; and, in a sure sign that he had made it big time, a sit down on 60 Minutes with Mike Wallace.

All the while, hundreds of thousands of fundraising letters from the organized Jewish community were being sent out to people like me asking for a donation, to help combat "The rising tide of anti-semitism in the black community."

A joke circulated among my fellow journalists at that time, whispered quietly, of course: "Ah hah, say something Jews don't like – that's how to become famous."

While we knew that Farrakhan was guilty as charged of not thinking much of Jews, most of us, however, deeply resented the suggestion that he spoke for us, and that a large army of anti-semites was running amok in the African American community. We knew that nothing could have been further from the truth; that most blacks didn't even know what a semite was, and Jews were just plain "white folks," enjoying all the many privileges that white folks traditionally have enjoyed in this country, and nothing more.

We said nothing, although we felt that our community was being unfairly defamed in the name of fundraising, because what was unspoken among us was naked fear. We, who once faced down heavily armed nightriders with nothing but our conviction that America should become a true democracy, now understood that what we were now faced with, real or imagined, was a new brand of white folks, whose principal weapons were not guns and the rope, but name calling, media influence, an acute awareness of where the levers of political power are located and tons of money.

We knew, again, real or imagined, that this power meant the loss of a job, standing in the community and being made a social pariah, unfit for human company.

It is this same fear that is at the heart of the Israel lobby.

Despite all the innuendos surrounding this book, of dark Protocols of the Learned Elders of Zion type of secret cabals and hidden conspiracy, most of the "what" in The Israel Lobby is fairly common knowledge—at least to those people who look beyond Entertainment Tonight and In Touch magazine for their information.

For example, it's hardly a closely held secret that Israel is the largest recipient of America's foreign aid. As the authors point out, "as of 2005, direct U.S. economic and military assistance amounted to nearly $154 billion....the aid that the United States provides to several of Israel's neighbors is at least partly intended to benefit Israel as well. Egypt and Jordan are the number two and three recipients of U.S. foreign aid, but most of the money should be seen as a reward for good behavior—specifically, their willingness to sign peace treaties with Israel."

All this, as they also point out, for a prosperous, modern industrial power with a population a little less than New York City.

And, are we to be surprised that the political positions of the neoconservatives are the same as Benjamin Netanyahu's Likud party. Or that the American Israel Public Affairs Committee (AIPAC) is "without question the most effective lobby in Congress." Or that no one running for high public office will question our unconditional support for Israel.

"What explains this behavior?" the authors ask. "Why is there so little disagreement among the presidential hopefuls regarding Israel, when there are profound disagreements among them on almost every other important issue facing the United States, and when it is apparent that America's Middle East policy has gone badly awry?"

Professors Mearsheimer and Walt soon answer their own question. Because the Israel lobby has gradually become one of the most powerful interest groups in the country, candidates for high office pay close attention to its wishes. The individuals care deeply about Israel, and they do not want American politicians to criticize it, even when criticism might be warranted and might even be in Israel's best interest. Instead, these groups want the U.S. leaders to treat Israel as if it were the fifty-first state. Democrats and Republicans alike fear the lobby's clout. They all know that any politician who challenges its policies stands little chance of becoming president."

Anyone who has followed the recent so-called presidential "debates" knows full well the truth of that statement.

But again, all of this is well known. What is not as well-known is not the "what," but the "how," and the "why." And that is what is most deeply disturbing about this book.

The writers make clear that the Israel lobby is doing nothing underhanded nor illegal. Hundreds of lobbyists are doing the same thing every day. The only difference is that the Israel lobby has so far been better at what they do than anyone else. And, whatever else one thinks of the results, one can't help but admire—as we follow the path of the arguments the authors put forth—the sheer brilliance of the Israel lobby and its intelligent, sober, systematic application of knowledge, organization, discipline, money and single-mindedness to work its will on the American government, and the American public.

But one pauses when professors Mearsheimer and Walt make the most provocative statement in *The Israel Lobby* over and over again, the major theme in this book that is sure to leave readers' hair standing up in both America and Israel: "Backing Israel may have yielded strategic benefits in the past, but the benefits have declined sharply in recent years while the economic and diplomatic costs have increased. Instead of being a strategic asset, in fact, Israel has become a strategic liability for the United States.

Backing Israel so strongly is making Americans more vulnerable—not less—and making it harder for the United States to achieve important and urgent foreign policy goals."

In addition, later in the book they make another startling statement in regards to the Palestinian-Israel conflict, which is at the heart of the problems in the Middle East: "The United States has enormous potential leverage at its disposal for dealing with Israel and the Palestinians. It could threaten to cut off all economic and diplomatic support for Israel. If that were not enough, it would have little difficulty lining up international support to isolate Israel, much the way South Africa was singled out and shunned at the end of the last century."

Mearsheimer and Walt positions regarding Israel can't get any clearer than that, and we are certainly not used to hearing opinions like that expressed in America. Apparently, the fear of being called an anti-semite isn't what it used to be.

Despite the pair's strong feelings and the plan, they lay out for what could be done to counter the Israel lobby, at the end the reader may suspect that it is a little like closing the barn door after the old gray mare has already run off, to use an old-fashioned cliché—that nothing really can, or will be done about the "corrosive" affect of the Israel lobby.

If this is true, all it means is, because of the cumulative effect of money and highly motivated single-issue groups on the democratic process, that the American people, in effect, have lost their democracy. For example, all polls indicate that most Americans not only hate illegal immigration with a passion, but most also would like to see a slowdown in legal immigration. But pressure and money from business and special interest groups have in effect, erased the American border and have declared that this is a "universal economic opportunity," and not really a country, and anyone who can get here, anywhere in the world, should be welcomed with open arms.

You would think that such a dramatic ending of the notion of the United States being an independent nation state with a culture, a history and borders to defend would at least be put to a vote. And is it any wonder that the vast majority of Americans now hold the Congress and the office of the President in such low esteem for betraying us so?

Now, in our Brave New World, Americans cannot help but conclude, especially after reading a book like *The Israeli Lobby*, and reading how all segments of our government all grovel in mortal fear, and bow down to the awesome power of lobbyists—that there is now a new sheriff in town, and his last name isn't Smith, or Jones, but sometimes goes by the moniker pesos, or euros, or most common, dollars; and his message is blunt, and to the point: "My way, or the highway."

Some of My Best Friends are Black: The Strange Story of Integration in America

By Tanner Colby

An Essay by Fred Beauford

The Strange Story of Integration in America

Some of My Best Friends Are Black

TANNER COLBY
author of THE CHRIS FARLEY SHOW

Integration: A Personal Journey

That lone black kid in the class on the cover photo of Tanner Colby's book, *Some of My Best Friends are Black: The Strange Story of Integration in America,* was me for many years, until the age of fourteen, so his book was deeply personal.

The more I read and thought about Tanner's book, however, the more I realized that the basic content he presented is nothing new to me. Jim Sleeper's *Closet of Strangers* and *Liberal Racism* and almost everything written by firebrand author Tim Wise, have gone over much of the territory

Colby is writing about. As a reporter and editor during some of the time period he covers, I had first-hand knowledge of much of what he writes about.

He covers the subject matter well, and I recommend this book, with few reservations.

In the end, for me, what makes *Some of My Best Friends are Black* intriguing, and come fully alive, was why he asked the question in the first place: "Why don't I know any black people?"

That question is rarely asked as far as I know, especially in Brooklyn, where he lived when he first asked himself that very question.

***

Tanner's story begins as a transplanted Southerner living in New York City, in Brooklyn, the place that we from the Bronx love to bash. He points out that he had descended "from poor white trash." And one day, this new New Yorker, who had long shaken off his four grandparents' grim fate as sharecroppers, woke up and realized that he didn't know any black people. This was a shock to his system. He asked around to friends and coworkers and they also did not know one black person.

He then takes us on a personal journey through white flight, busing, and affirmative action for white people, going back to places in the south where he grew up, to examine just how the structure of racial segregation between blacks and whites had been carefully maintained in America.

On the issue of redlining and affirmative action for white people, for example, he would inspire fellow white author Tim Wise to stand up and cheer, as he points out that "After the war, the heroes of Normandy and Okinawa were duly rewarded by their country. The GI Bill gave low-interest, zero-percent-down mortgages to all returning servicemen. In truth, GI loans were simply FHA loans by another name, subject to the same redlining restrictions. When the whites of the "Greatest Generation" went looking for a place to call home, it was all but illegal for them to buy a home in a subdivision that didn't exclude blacks. Black veterans, on the other hand, could use their housing vouchers only in all-black areas; even with the GI Bill, many were still denied loans.

"In the history of race, slavery and segregation are always called out for what they did to blacks' human and civil rights. Redlining and racial covenants never seem to get the same amount of play, despite the damage they did to blacks' property rights. We get to act like all that money out in the suburbs came from nothing but hard work, and not a big, fat, racist handout from Uncle Sam.

"The suburban land grab of the twentieth century was one of the single greatest engines of wealth creation in human history. It took a country of second-and third-generation white ethnic immigrants, vaulted them into the middle class, and sent all their kids to college."

Tanner's book also includes the large role Black Nationalism played in keeping America a segregated country. "Well before the 1960s stumbled to a close," he writes, faith in Martin Luther King Jr.'s idealistic, integrationist crusade had waned." Blacks started calling for "Black Power," and the Black Consciousness Movement was born. Some whites were shocked to learn that a great many blacks wanted nothing to do with them, and integration was seen as "insidious subterfuge for the maintenance of white supremacy."

Not to mention (as I have pointed out in a review of *Is Marriage for White People?),* all of that carrying on between black men and white women that had suddenly started in the mid-'60s was seen by many blacks as something that did not bode well for the black community.

Tanner is both courageous and astute in pointing out that this was fool's gold, and was mainly led by a small group of people grasping for the few affirmative action dollars available, while helping to destroy hope that blacks could compete in the larger mainstream, all in the name of black pride.

Pointing to the rise of a handful of black advertising companies, he writes: "In the Sixties, civil rights groups had demanded that Madison Avenue abandon its grotesque stereotypes of black America and create integrated racially neutral advertisements. In the era of black power and black pride, black leaders and agencies now reversed course.... After years of telling mainstream agencies that they had to market to black America, black agencies were now saying that mainstream agencies *couldn't* market to black America; only black agencies were qualified to do that. And in making their stand as experts on black culture, the black agencies only cemented the institutional bias that had kept them out of the industry in the first place: if only black people can sell to black people, then surely only white people can sell to white people—and white people were the lion's share of the market."

What came to mind when I read this is remembering that one of the key arguments the Black Nationalists made back then was what they saw as the Jewish example of total community solidarity. I wondered, as I did then, what it would have been like for the Jewish community today, if Jewish filmmakers, after they gained control over the fledgling film industry from the Edison Trust in 1914, had proceeded to make movies only for Jews, in the name of Jewish pride. Would they today be one of richest and most feared group in America? I think not.

***

The move back into the cities nationwide by young, college-educated whites has been well noted. New York City, for example, has been drawing them in unheard of numbers. The awesome expansion of university systems like New York University and the New School into world-class institutions, Mayor Giuliani formerly having run most of the low-lifes out of town, Wall Street stealing everything from around the world that wasn't locked down—an amazing transformation has started taking place.

Once, people like Tanner would have received their degrees, had a few beers, and headed back to the suburbs. No longer. They now want to live in a place like Brooklyn, the new East Village, the new home of writers, creative types of all kind, and bona fide hipsters.

Yet the real Brooklyn they encountered on a daily basis is also home to a vast majority of people who have formed into unbroachable racial and religious blocs, have lived right next to each other for over a hundred years, and never once said "hi."

What's interesting about this new group of immigrants pouring into Brooklyn, and immigrants they are, is that they are Americans, and they thought that they knew what being an American was.

Now that they have decided to stay, are these newcomers, whose grandparents fled places like Brooklyn in headlong white flight, going to try and shape it in a different way by creating a different kind of Brooklyn?

Brooklyn seems to be the inspiration for the young Mr. Tanner to ask the question: "Why don't I know any Blacks?"

The Color of War: How One Battle Broke Japan and Another Changed America

By James Campbell

An essay by Fred Beauford

American History 101

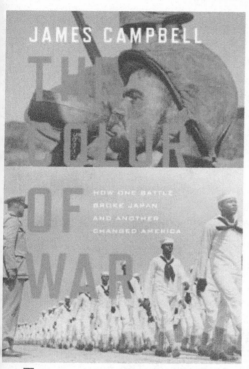

From the very first, I thought author James Campbell had a brilliant

insight when he decided to marry the story of the horrific event that

occurred on July 17, 1944, at the Port Chicago Naval Magazine in Port

Chicago, California, and one month earlier, the gruesome and bloody invasion of Saipan, an important island in the Marianas chain, in the War in the Pacific.

As I finished the book, however, I noted that he never alluded to my idea anywhere in his book: what happened to the black sailors at Port Chicago was the same mindset that led up to 52 million losing their lives, as the tribal conflict that began in earnest in 1914, where casualties, in the end, were over 35 million—restarted with little regard for human life.

Adolf Hitler's praise of America in *Mein Kampf* wasn't for nothing.

Here are the basic facts: The bombardment. of Saipan began on the 13th of June 1944. Fifteen battleships were involved, and 165,000 shells were fired.

The landings began at 7 a.m. on the 15th of June 1944. More than 300 LVTs landed 8,000 marines on the west coast of Saipan by about 9 a.m. Eleven fire support ships covered the marine landings. The naval force consisted of battleships, cruisers and destroyers.

The invasion surprised the Japanese high command, which had been expecting an attack further south. Admiral Soemu Toyoda, commander-in-chief of the Japanese Navy, saw an opportunity to use the A-Go force to attack the U.S. Navy forces around Saipan. On the 15th of June, he gave the order to attack. But the resulting battle of the Philippine Sea was a disaster for the Imperial Japanese Navy, which lost three aircraft carriers and hundreds of planes. The garrisons of the Marianas would have no hope of resupply or reinforcement.

By July 7th, the Japanese on Saipan had nowhere to retreat and made a final suicidal banzai charge. At dawn, with a group of 12 men carrying a great red flag in the lead, the remaining able-bodied troops—about 3,000 men—charged forward in the final attack. Amazingly, behind them came the wounded, with bandaged heads, crutches, and barely armed. The Japanese surged over the American front lines, engaging both army and marine units. The 1st and 2nd Battalions of the 105th U.S. Infantry were almost destroyed, with 650 killed and wounded. However, the fierce resistance of these two battalions, as well as that of the Headquarters Company, 105th Infantry, elements of 3rd Battalion, and 10th Marines (an artillery unit) resulted in over 4,300 Japanese killed. This was the largest Japanese Banzai attack in the Pacific War.

By 4:15 pm on the 9th of July, it was announced that Saipan was officially secured. In the end, almost the entire garrison of Japanese troops on the island—at least 30,000—died. For the Americans, the victory was the costliest to date in the Pacific War, with 2,949 Americans killed and 10,464 wounded, out of the 71,000 who landed.

***

The Port Chicago disaster was a deadly munitions explosion occurred at the Port Chicago Naval Magazine in Port Chicago, Calif., in the San Francisco Bay Area. Campbell likened it to a "small atomic explosion." Munitions detonated while being loaded onto a cargo vessel bound for the Pacific Theater of Operations, killing 320 sailors and civilians and injuring 390 others. Most of the dead and injured were enlisted African-American sailors.

A month later, continuing unsafe conditions inspired hundreds of servicemen to refuse to load munitions, an act known as the Port Chicago Mutiny. Fifty African American men—called the "Port Chicago 50"—were convicted of mutiny and sentenced to long prison terms. Forty-seven of the 50 were released in January 1946; the remaining three served additional months in prison.

During and after the trial, questions were raised about the fairness and legality of the court-martial proceedings. Due to public pressure, the United States Navy reconvened the courts-martial board in 1945 and the court affirmed the guilt of the convicted men. Widespread publicity surrounding the case turned it into a cause célèbre among both African Americans and white Americans; it and other race-related Navy protests of 1944–1945 led the Navy to change its practices and initiate the desegregation of its forces beginning in February 1946. In 1994, the Port Chicago Naval Magazine National Memorial was dedicated to the lives lost in the disaster.

***

Campbell makes these facts come fully alive by following the personal stories of a few young recruits, both black and white as they lived through all the horrors of all-out war and racial discrimination.

But it is this racial discrimination that is the heart and soul of *The Color of War* and makes it not just another book about the horrors of war. Campbell makes us see firsthand just how seriously all major institutions in America were dedicated to oppressing black people, including the military, with the Navy and the Marine Corps. being the most egregious.

Writes Campbell," The truth was that although every branch of service desperately needed men, neither the Army nor the Marines nor the Navy wanted black men. Hoping to stave off the entrance of blacks, every branch of service seized upon an Army War College Report on 'The Use of Negro Manpower in War.' 'In the process of evolution,' the report stipulated, 'the American Negro has not progressed as far as other subspecies of the human family...The cranial cavity of the Negro is smaller than whites...The psychology of the Negro, based on heredity derived from mediocre African ancestors, cultivated by generations of slavery, is one from which we cannot expect to draw leadership material...In general the Negro is jolly, docile, tractable, and lively but with harsh or unkind treatment can become stubborn, sullen and unruly. In physical courage, he falls well back of whites...He is most susceptible to 'Crowd Psychology.' He cannot control himself in fear of danger...He is a rank coward in the dark."

Obviously, black leaders became incensed when the report leaked out, and far from being docile, this only made them increase their pressure on President Roosevelt. Civil Rights organizations, including the union leader A. Philip Randolph, threatened FDR with a proposed gigantic March on Washington in 1941. Randolph and other black leaders were blessed with the help of a nationwide, lively and outspoken black press and most importantly, the constant lobbying of First Lady Eleanor Roosevelt, black America's closest white friend, to get President Roosevelt to issue Executive Order 8802 barring discrimination in defense industries and federal bureaus (the Fair Employment Act), forcing these services to allow blacks to serve as more than valets and cooks.

Campbell handles all of this with great skill.

***

Although the battle for Saipan was a major turning point in the War in the Pacific, it is overshadowed in the history of who was going to control this vast amount of water by the battle of Iwo Jima a year later, where the 2,949 Americans killed and 10,464 wounded on Saipan seemed almost like a minor sideshow compared to the 6,821 Marines killed and 19,217 wounded on Iwo Jima, the most that organization ever experienced in a single engagement.

***

As far as the incident at Port Chicago, it has also been largely lost to history. We are indebted to James Campbell for once more bringing both to light.

Infamy: The Shocking Story of the Japanese American Internment in World War Two

By Richard Reeves

Reviewed by Fred Beauford

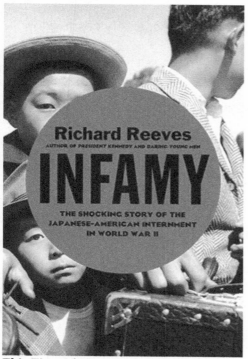

This Time It's Personal

For a number of years I ran a small café (Fred's Café) and bookstore at the Sunday Hollywood Farmer's Market on Ivar, between Hollywood and Sunset boulevards.

I was then a member of the Ivar Theater, now owned by the Inner City Cultural Center, an organization I worked for over two decades.

The Ivar Theater was then the most prominent structure on the two blocks, and we had voted to allow the farmers to use our restrooms on Sunday.

But someone had to be there by 6:30 a.m. to let everybody in. Theater people are not noted for being early risers. So, as the only writer on the board of directors, I was the one everyone pointed at.

So what? Unlike those actors and actresses and directors, the night offered little for me. I loved getting up early.

My little café and bookstore did well, and I made many friends. One day, the friendly lady who sold me those delicious Fuji apples, came out of the restroom, stopped, and pointed to a new book on sale, *Farewell to Manzanar*, by Jeanne Wakatsuk Houston and James Houston.

"See that little girl in that picture on the cover, that's me."

I didn't know what to say. But, from that brief statement became a lesson in a history that I knew nothing about: the forced internment of Japanese Americans in concentration camps in World War II, which Richard Reeves covers with remarkable writing skills, excellent research and a voice much like the voice that was running through my head as the friendly apple seller over time told me her harrowing tale, which *Infamy* well documents.

Reeves makes an important point early in his book: "Living in California on and off for years, I've passed Manzanar many times, each time thinking I should stop; each time thinking I should write about what happened there and in the other camps in Arizona, Colorado, Wyoming, Utah, and Arkansas. I am from a part of the country, New York, where most of the people I know had only the vaguest notion that these events happened."

He had that right. This rube from the Bronx was one of those "educated" New Yorkers who knew nothing about these camps. Concentration camps were for Nazis, not Americans.

After the attack of Pearl Harbor on December 7, 1941, attention was immediately focused on the Japanese living among us, most of whom lived on the West Coast, with California having the largest number. The FBI started raiding homes, detaining at will any Japanese American they deemed worthy of investigation.

Some of this was driven by the notion that they were different, inassimilable. As the Commanding Officer of the Western Defense Command, Lieutenant General John DeWitt said often, "A Jap is a Jap."

The press and the politicians whipped the American public into a wild frenzy over this potential "Fifth Column." Among these are historic names that I was shocked to find.

As Reeves point out: "The villains of this story include California Attorney General Earl Warren, who rode the anti-Japanese tide to the governorship of California; Secretary of State Cordell Hull; Secretary of War Henry Stimson; Assistant Secretary of war John McCloy; Roger Baldwin, the hypocritical founder of the American Civil Liberties Union; Supreme Court justices Tom Clark and William O. Douglas; as well as William Randolph Hearst, Walter Lippmann, Edward R. Murrow, and hundreds of other raving journalists."

In addition, there was the land grab of the greedy whites that coveted Japanese businesses and especially the farms they so skillfully managed.

Writes Reeves: "Whatever goodwill there was for Issei and Nisei after Pearl Harbor was soon gone as news arrived daily of seemingly invincible and brutal Japanese armies running wild through the Philippines, Burma, Hong Kong, Malaya, and the Dutch East Indies. Tolerance of any kind was replaced by fear and by the greed of white merchants and farmers who wanted to eliminate competition from California's 6,000 Japanese-operated farms, which totaled at least 250,000 acres and were worth more than $75 million. More than 40 percent of California's produce was from American Japanese farms that often stood on land white farmers ignored as too poor for cultivation.

"In the cities. Many white businessmen coveted the stores, businesses, and fishing boats of Japanese competitors."

I should add that it wasn't just the "greedy whites" that benefited from the internment of the Japanese Americans; but, as my friend, the apple seller, pointed out to me, that many of those nice homes black Americans were now living in in South Central Los Angeles, were once owned by Japanese Americans.

When the roundup came they were given just 24 hours to get everything in order and could only take what they could carry. Their houses and businesses and property went for a song.

***

In addition, there was also a Colonel Adolf Eichmann type, lurking, who provided the legal groundwork for sending the Japanese Americans to concentration camps: Colonel Karl Bendetsen.

Author Reeves has absolutely no use for this man, who was "a brilliant pathological liar, drove the process, grossly exaggerating the dangers posed by West Coast Japanese."

In one of the great ironies, given what was happening in Germany at the same time to Jews, Colonel Bendetsen was from a prominent Orthodox

Jewish family that had emigrated from Lithuania. and his last name was Bendetson.

"But in 1929 he denied all that, claiming to be a Christian to get into a Stanford fraternity, Theta Delta Chi, which barred Jews from membership. As the years went by, he created a new biography under the name Bendetsen, saying that he was from a Danish logging family and that a fictional great-grandfather had come from Denmark to America in 1670," writes Reeves.

***

All of this set the stage for one of the most infamous acts in American history as on February 19, 1942, President Roosevelt, feeling pressure from wherever he turned, signed Executive Order 9066, which resulted in the mass incarceration of 120,000 West Coast American Japanese.

***

We see how all of this plays out in Richard Reeves' wonderful book *Infamy*. This, however, is not a pleasant book to read. There is just too much suffering. But the book does speak profoundly to the *idea* of America, whether the author realized it or not.

Most of the Japanese Americans faced their unfair fate with much fortitude because they deeply believed in the idea of America, not the America that then existed.

My friend, the apple seller, at the Hollywood Farmer's Market, taught me that.

This is a must-read book.

Detroit: An American Autopsy
By Charlie LeDuff
An essay by Fred Beauford

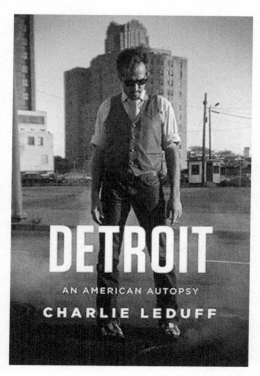

The New World

I have only been to Detroit twice. The first time I had a grand time with two of my daughters, both preteens. It was in 1991 and I was the Editorial Director of the *Crisis* magazine, the official publication of the NAACP.

Detroit was the NAACP's kind of town. Coleman Young was the longtime first black mayor, he and welcomed us with opened arms; the new Renaissance Center was booming. The hotel we stayed in on the famed Waterfront, with a view of Canada, right across the river, was first rate, and rivaled any of the many big, medium and small city hotels we had stayed at, as we held our convention each year.

And the plus was that Detroit had one of the largest urban memberships of the NAACP than anywhere in the United States; and the local chapter's annual Freedom Fund Dinner, was *the* social event of the year for blacks of notoriety in Detroit, and it brought us much needed income.

Most importantly, for me at least, everyone at the convention had read or heard of *The Crisis.*

To be sure, there was much seriousness of purpose at this convention, especially given all the many deadly serious problems blacks faced in America, and especially in Detroit. Still, there was also plenty of time for back slapping, loud laughter, dancing all night, and general carrying on, and enjoying each other's company.

My two girls were all excited, loving the experience, and seeing their dad in a friendly, showoff mode.

These annual conventions were something I always looked forward to, and this year in the famed city of Detroit, it didn't disappoint. Even Jack Kemp, then in charge of HUD under Bush the First, showed up.

***

Years later, in 2005, Rob Morton, CEO of Morton Books, Inc., sent me back to Detroit, this time to help organized a book party for a new author, and carry the Morton Books banner.

And this is where I encountered the Detroiter Charlie LeDuff, who writes so well about in his grim theater of the absurd in *Detroit: An American Autopsy.*

I was driven down desolated street after street, as a Morton Books author, a retired African American school teacher, gave me warning after warning about these deadly streets.

This was a far cry from the fancy Renaissance Center, and the rest of the riverfront, with its statue of the famous Joe Louis, who once lived in Detroit, guarding the entry.

And where were those well-dressed blacks, and that small spattering of liberal whites I had so much fun with at the NAACP annual convention?

They were nowhere to be seen on these empty, gloomy, ghostlike streets I was staring out on in disbelief. I had never seen anything like this before.

LeDuff , a former *New York Times* and *Detroit News* feature writer, is a native son of Detroit driven by family demons, but he could not help but return to his hometown, even as it was on the brink of total chaos.

He is the descendant of French Cajuns from Louisiana, Native Americans, hillbillies and, as he discovered only a few years ago, by chance, the first LeDuffs to reach Detroit from Louisiana were classified by the census as M for mixed race. That M was quickly replaced as W as soon as they landed in Detroit.

These were the people, along with huge numbers of real blacks, part of the largest internal immigration in American history, escaping finally, from their imprisonment in the South—who flocked to Detroit, all hearing the beckoning call of hard work and high wages.

***

Henry Ford is not my favorite American Capitalist because of his innovation of the assembly line in large-scale manufacturing, but because he was the first of the Robber Barons that had that eureka idea: If I pay my workers a decent wage, then they can buy my product.

Hummm.

As LeDuff points out, the good times started rolling after Ford's brilliant, but obvious, insight, and Detroit became the richest city in America.

"Detroit" he writes, "in the nineteenth century was the center of the nation's carriage and wheel and stove industries because of its lumber and the rich ore in the upper reaches of Michigan. This set the stage for tinkerers like Ransom Olds, who was among the nation's largest carriage manufacturers before he turned to cars. Henry Ford, a farmer, built his first automobile in Highland Park in 1899. Detroit would rapidly become the world's machine shop, its factory, growing in population from 300,000 to 1.3 million in the twenty-five years following Ford's grand opening."

Here, LeDuff quotes the British politician and author Ramsay Muir, who in 1925 sniffed, "It is the home of mass production, very high wages and colossal profits, of reckless installment buying and shifting labor surplus. It regards itself as the temple of a new gospel of progress to which I will give the name Detroitism."

To be sure.

Workers didn't need much education and ingenious ideas like easy credit and the layaway plan was offered to them by the carmakers.

***

I read page after page of LeDuff's riveting, heated prose, part autobiography, including his often-harrowing experiences as a reporter for the *Detroit News.* It was stylistically a cross between Jimmy Breslin and Ernest Hemingway, of murder, political and business malfeasance and cluelessness, race baiting and just sheer hopelessness and despair.

I kept thinking of, as I turned page after page, of all things, San Francisco.

This line of thought started after I read this from our author of how his friends and family regarded life as the big change was about to descend on them, as the Japanese had learned to make better cars, cheaper than Detroit, and everyone in the world would soon know it.

"Nobody bothered to get educated," he writes. "My sister and brothers and Carrie and Doc and too many others dropped out of high school, yet nobody went to work in the automobile plants. You suspected the work was too hard and the union made the work too hard to get."

San Francisco, and the entire Bay Area, was also undergoing a transition from its blue collar roots around the same time, as thousands of well-paid dock workers, who did the back-breaking work of loading and unloading giant ships, had been displaced by the rise of the container ship.

Yet, San Francisco, and the Bay Area, had something else in its collective DNA: North Beach, which nurtured the Beats; writers, thinkers and visionaries lurking in seedy dives and garages, bolstered by two world-class universities, UC Berkeley and Stanford.

When the time came for San Franciscans and Bay Area folks to readapt, to change from brawn to brains, they more than rose to the occasion and created Apple, Silicon Valley and the modern gee wiz electronic world we live in today.

That great two-bedroom apartment in the Upper Mission overlooking the East Bay, I had for a song when I was a visiting professor at Berkeley in the 80s, would now cost me $4,500, if I was lucky.

Detroit was not so lucky, as LeDuff's book testifies to. Today, in Detroit, you can't even give apartments like that away.

The Triple Package: How Three Unlikely Traits Explain the Rise and Fall of Cultural Groups in America.

By Amy Chua and Jed Rubenfeld

Reviewed by Fred Beauford

Let the Generalizations Begin

What is authors Amy Chua and Jed Rubenfeld—one a Chinese

American, the other, a Jewish American, both Yale Law School professors

and married to each, with two daughters—big idea, or, as is the case, big

ideas?

They insist in *Triple Package: How Three Unlikely Traits Explain the Rise and Fall of Cultural Groups in America*, using a great number of academic studies and anecdotal evidence to backup this claim, that certain groups rise in this country because they process The Triple Package of an ingrained Superiority Complex; Insecurity because of the belief that the WASP majority looks down on them, and don't consider them real Americans, which gives them a "chip on their shoulders"; and Impulse Control, where strict self-discipline prevails.

It goes without saying that group solidarity is the glue that holds all of this together.

The religious and racial groups they cite include Chinese, Jews, Mormons, Nigerians, Cubans, Iranians, Indians and Lebanese. What all of these groups have in common is that most of the people in these groups are recent immigrants to this country, starting with the lifting of restrictions that favored certain kinds of Northern Europeans that ended in the '60s (thank Senator Edward Kennedy for helping make that happen) with the exception of the Mormons and the Jews, both German and Eastern European.

Many Chinese Americans, which strangely, they didn't note, have also been in this country for many decades, and were the essential key to the building of the western part of the intercontinental railroad system in the 1860s.

This is also not the first book that has traveled down this road. For example, Thomas Sowell, the black conservative Stanford University economist made similar points in a more concise way in his 1981 book, *Ethnic America: A History*.

***

Although Chua and Rubenfeld offer interesting profiles of these "rising" groups, in the end, it is their insights into the Chinese and Jewish personalities that dwarf anything they write about the other groups, and it is why this reader realized early on that this book was not just some dry academic study as was professor Sowell's book.

***

This was also personal. Almost as if the authors said, if I show you mine, will you show me yours, which made this book almost impossible to put down.

***

With the insights they have at hand, Chua and Jed Rubenfeld have concluded that what the rest of these striving groups have in common with the Chinese and Jews, is the ability to see their group as better than anyone else, with tons of history to back up that claim; to study hard; put in long hours at whatever line of work they decide on (work that must carry with it prestige, and lots and lots of money). They also are people who closely follow the time-honored rules of the group (the collective unbroken genetic memory) and resist the temptations to accede to a broader American culture.

As they point out, "America today spreads a message of immediate gratification, living for the moment. ...Americans are taught that no group is superior to another in any respect...Americans are taught that self-esteem—feeling good about yourself—is the key to a successful life."

The groups they are writing about will have none of this. For them, it is about money, power and pleasing your parents.

Jewish, Inc. Chinese, Inc. Nigerian, Inc. will always trump the myth of two-fisted individualism any day.

In fact, Thomas Sowell, agrees with them. Or, maybe they agree with Professor Sowell.

I couldn't argue with their basic idea because the evidence is there. Jews are far and away the wealthiest people in America. Followed by most of the groups they mention. The once dominant WASP are now mere shadows of their former mighty selves.

What I did find questionable is how they tried to paint New World groups with the same brush as Old World people.

For example, in their treatment of the so-called Hispanics, they seem to not fully understand why most Cubans hate being lumped in with Mexicans, Puerto Ricans, and Santa Dominicans.

What they also don't seem to know is that most Mexicans also dislike being called Hispanic, or Latino.

I should know.

My ex is part Mexican and I have gotten earfuls at the dinner table from her large family about how "you guys" are the illegals, and they have been in this part of the world at least 12,000 years. They also took serious exception at being considered Spanish.

The Cubans that fled Castro were the white elite. Cuba was the second to last country in the Western Hemisphere to abolish slavery. This occurred in 1886, followed by Brazil in 1888.

It wasn't just that these exiles considered Castro a closet communist, which proved to be the case, but also the fact that he said that blacks were equal citizens of Cuba.

For them, that was unforgivable.

This lumping of all of all these people together is mostly for political reasons and has no basis in any kind of group affinity.

And speaking of blacks, they also trotted out the argument for separate but equal for African Americans as a way for economic attainment, giving more face time to the early version of Malcolm X when he was in the Nation of Islam, than to the latter Malcolm X who turned his back on his old ideas.

Martin Luther King, Jr., with his idea of integration, was not even worth discussing in any length.

But again, I smelled Old World people trying to lump New World people in the only box they know. Try as they may to prove otherwise, the fact is that most African Americans are not Africans with an unbroken genetic memory like the Chinese and Jews.

The One Drop Rule was a grim fairy tale, enforced by the English settlers at the point of a gun because they wanted to hold their mixed-race offspring in bondage, as Thomas Jefferson did.

Here is what another law professor, Ralph Richard Banks of Stanford wrote in his recent book, *Is Marriage For White People?*: "For most of American history, the question of whether a black woman's children would be black was a nonstarter…that was done by the so-called one drop rule…according to this principle, reflected in social practice and law alike, one drop of black blood was sufficient to make a person black. In the infamous 1896 case of Plessey v. Ferguson, for example, the fact that seven out of Homer Plessey's eight great-grandparents were white was not sufficient to allow him to sit in the white railroad car in segregated Louisiana.'"

As law professors at a school like Yale, I would have expected our two authors to know this and add this to their analysis of African American, as well as know that, starting in the '60s most interracial children were raised by their white mothers, which was perhaps the most radical change that has occurred in American history.

African Americans are New World people, and our story is just now being written, if we can just avoid Old World typecasting.

***

Still, the *Triple Package* was often one of the most riveting books I have read so far this year, mainly because the authors, bravely in my opinion, faced up the negative consequences of the *Triple Package*, and didn't shy away from seeing the dangers inherent in the three traits they claim helped the groups they mentioned gain so much economic power in this country.

As the two authors focused their attention, and zeroed in on both the Chinese and Jewish populations, something they know both intellectually, and most important, emotionally—we get enormous insight into both groups, and the price they pay for the direction they embarked on centuries ago.

For the Chinese, it is an overbearing culture based on denial, hard work, self-control, and above all, conformity.

A Confucian principle, which still guides many Chinese, teaches that the goal of life is for the good of the group, not of the individual. (Ayn Rand was clearly not a Confucian); they also have to deal with learning by rote, which could end up only suiting them for exact science where two and two is four, with no questions asked.

The authors are aware of this, as well as many in China and the Chinese in America. Recently, in the Bay Area, for example, Chinese business people held a large conference because it was impossible to no longer ignore the fact that although Chinese students now dominate the numbers at UC Berkeley and Stanford, two of the most elite universities in the world, that when they graduate, often with honors, and enter the work world, they rarely rise out of middle management at major corporations in the Bay Area.

They concluded that this was not due to racism, but culture.

"Speak up! Take chances!" one angry businessman shouted to the mainly Chinese American audience.

***

This book gives us many insights into the inner dimensions Chinese Americans face, and I was glad to see that the authors face it directly, and with almost brutal honesty.

***

The Jews also have their own challenges to bear. Despite their being, by almost any measure, the most successful Old World group in America, they are still haunted by deep-seeded insecurities, according to the authors. For example, they note that "Jews are also awkwardly prominent in Hollywood, a fact that many Jews prefer not to highlight."

They dislike having this fact discussed with such passion that a non-Jew could be labeled anti-Semitic for writing the same quote you just read.

In addition, they question the idea that a single-minded pursuit for money and power is a productive way to spend one's life. For them, a single-minded focus on money and power could lead Jews into some dangerous waters.

Professors Chua and Rubenfeld are not alone in this observation. There is a recent, soul-searching editorial by Rob Eshman in the *Los Angeles Jewish Journal* in regard to the movie, *The Wolf of Wall Street*. "But, just between us (and one lone African American listening in), let's talk about Belfort-the-Jew — let's go there. In the movie, you never really understand how someone so gifted can be so morally unmoored. But in his memoir, upon which the movie is based, whenever Belfort refers to his Jewish roots, the diagnosis becomes more apparent.

He is a kid from Long Island. His dad, Max, grew up "in the old Jewish Bronx, in the smoldering economic ashes of the Great Depression. Belfort didn't grow up poor by any means, he just wasn't rich enough. The hole in him wasn't from poverty, but from the desire for acceptance. The "blue-blooded WASPs," Belfort writes, "viewed me as a young Jewish circus attraction."

"Belfort had a chip on his shoulder the size of a polo pony, and so did everyone he recruited They were, he writes, "the most savage young Jews anywhere on Long Island: the towns of Jericho and Syosset. It was from out of the very marrow of these two upper-middle-class Jewish ghettos that the bulk of my first hundred Strattonites had come...."

"It's not complicated, really. Poor little Jordan wanted to show those WASPs whose country clubs he couldn't join that he was smarter, richer, better. What he failed to understand is that just about every Jew, every minority, shares the same impulses. But only a select few decide the only way to help themselves is to hurt others.

"Belfort, like Bernie Madoff, is an extreme example. These are guys who feel they have nothing, they *are* nothing, so they will do anything to acquire everything. They cross a pretty clear line and just keep going.

"The question that gnaws at me is whether there's something amiss in the vast gray area that leads right up to that line. Are the Belforts and Madoffs unnatural mutations, or are they inevitable outgrowths of attitudes that have taken root in our communities?"

***

If there is anything that can prove that they make good points in their book, *The Triple Package*, it is that editorial in the *Jewish Journal*.

Herbie Hancock: Possibilities

With Lisa Dickey

Reviewed by Fred Beauford

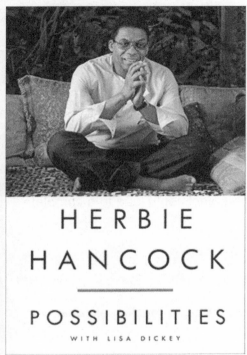

A most Interesting man

Herbie Hancock's *Possibilities* is, surprisingly, a more interesting look at the evolution of an American popular artist than what we have been used to.

Not only is the noble story of the upward mobility of a bright, highly talented young black American male from the South Side of Chicago, fully told, but there is also Herbie Hancock, a very thoughtful, self-aware, cerebral fellow, indeed.

He is also one of those rare birds who fly in a flock of his own making.

Here is how he describes himself early in the book: "This was how my brain worked. As a kid, I loved mechanics and science, and I spent hours taking apart clocks and toasters because I had a driving need to know how things worked. I was drawn to the rational order of these systems, enraptured by the way that taking apart an object could lead to a complete understanding of that object."

This acute curiosity about how things work extended to music, which led him to constant search for new ways to enhance the musical experience.

Now, Herbie Hancock wears the label "jazz legend," which means that he can now display bragging rights held by few, by pointing to his fourteen Grammys and an Oscar for the score of the film *Round Midnight*.

In addition, there was his being named in 2011 as an UNESCO Goodwill Ambassador, in 2013 he was a recipient of the Kennedy Center Honors, and in 2014 he became the first jazz musician to deliver the prestigious Norton Lectures at Harvard.

His musical education started at an early age while growing up on the South Side of 1950s Chicago. A friend of his who lived in his building had a piano. Hancock loved playing around with it so much that he prevailed upon his family to purchase him one.

"So when I was seven, they gave me a used piano they'd bought for about $5 in a church basement."

That old piano led to private music lesson, which led to young Herbie quickly being recognized as a child prodigy. At eleven, by dint of winning a young people's competition, he played a movement a Mozart piano concerto with the Chicago Symphony.

***

The pull between science and music, however, did not go away, and came to a head, when in the fall of 1956 at just sixteen, he entered Grinnell College, a small, overwhelmingly white, liberal arts school in Iowa.

Writes Hancock, "Even before I set foot on campus I started examining my options analytically. Should I major in music or in science? I loved them both, but I wanted to make the smart choice. So I asked myself *what are the chances you can make a living from jazz? Questionable. Now, what are the chances you can make a living from science? Probably really good.*

"As much as I loved jazz, I decided to take the pragmatic path and major in engineering. I even promised my mother, who wanted me to get a degree in something useful, that I wouldn't major in music."

And lucky for the world of music Hancock's pragmatism didn't last long, with his changing his major in his second year at the college, to music. His memoir then takes us on a long, fruitful musical journey, where at one point, he and I crossed paths.

In addition, much of this book also took a close look at the many technical innovations that has occurred in the production of both recorded and live music presentation, and how Hancock's love of science caused him to embrace these new, and often strange machines, long before other musicians.

This passage fully illustrates the point better than anything I could come up with. Writes Hancock, "The first record we made after I got the Apple 11+ was *Monster.*" Here's the listing in *Monster's* liner notes of what instruments he played:

Herbie Hancock: piano, E-MU Polyphonic keyboard, Clavitar, Waves Minimoog, Prophet-5, Oberheim 8 Voice, Yamaha CS-80, ARP 2600, Hohner D6 Clavinet, Rhodes 88 Suitcase piano, Steiner EVI, Sennheiser Vocoder, WLM Organ, Linn-Moffett Drum, Modified Apple 11 Plus Microcomputer, Roland CR-70.

Oy Vey!

What ever happened to poor Miles Davis and a few good side men, which was Hancock's first experience with a jazz band?

***

Our meeting came during the time he fully left his "space music" phase, and became funky. The PR firm I worked for had Columbia Records for a client, and I worked on his groundbreaking album, *Head Hunters.*

Jazz purist moaned and groaned and called him a sellout, but the public loved the album and it became his best seller ever.

Here is some dialogue he shared in his book about the success of that album when after a few weeks his manager called him:

"'Hi Herbie,'" he said. "'Quick question for you. How many copies of *Head Hunters* do you think we sold this week?'"

"'I don't know,'" I told him. 'A thousand? Two thousand?' I figured sales were probably similar to what they'd been for *Crossing* and *Sextant.*"

"'Nope,'" he said. "'Seventy-eight thousand.' I sat there for a moment, stunned. And then we both stared laughing."

(I could take some credit for this, but as I soon found out: in show business, the PR person only gets credit if the thing is a flop.)

***

Not all was always so bright for Hancock. His talent raised him to great heights, but his personal demons almost destroyed him. In addition, bad things also happened to someone closest to him. His sister Jean was killed in a plane crash at age forty-one, which was a hard blow for him to take.

But the real pain for him and his wife, Gigi and daughter Jessica, came in 1999, when one night he was at a party and someone asked him if he had ever smoked cocaine?

He had noticed people going into a room and when they came out, he noticed that they were somehow different. High, maybe?

For him the answer was immediate and unambiguous: "Nooo," I said. "I'm afraid to do anything like that."

For Hancock, who was a long-time recreational user of cocaine, there was a clear line between snorting cocaine and smoking it. "Crack cocaine." He tells us, "was a relatively new drug, but to my mind it fell on the same side of the line as heroin, which I would never touch."

But as the party went on and Hancock loosened up, his curious mind caught up with him, and he decided to give it a try.

"I was led down the hallway into the bedroom, where someone put a pipe in my mouth and lit it. 'Draw it in and hold it,' the person told me. I did. And when the high hit me, it was like nothing I'd ever felt. Crack overloads the pleasure center of your brain, hitting you with a wave of every pleasurable sensation you can imagine, physical and emotional; all at once. I closed my eyes and thought, *Oh shit. I should have never done this.* This stuff was obviously way too dangerous to mess with," he writes.

But mess with it he did: "Toward the end of 1999 things were getting out of control. I was smoking a lot now, and acting in ways I'd never acted before."

This included not looking after his wife after she had an asthma attack, missing his daughter's birthday party when she turned 30, and disappearing for days.

Finally, Gigi had had enough. "Herbie," she said to him, "I'm not going to watch you die. If you continue this way, you are going to have to move out. I made some calls, and here are the numbers for some rehab places. But I'm not going to force you. You have to do this for yourself."

Hancock got the message and booked himself into Hoag Memorial Hospital rehab services that night. But unlike other celebrities that go into rehab with the cameras rolling and flashes going off everywhere—no one knew, beside a handful of people.

"I never wanted anyone else to find out. And in fact, I never told another soul for years, until I decided to reveal my addiction and rehab in this book. I used a false name in rehab, and I don't want to say too much about the program. But I want to give credit to the doctors, nurses, and staff at Hoag, because they took care of me with grace and discretion. I'm sure that some of them realized who I was, but nobody ever revealed it," Hancock writes.

For the readers who know little about the how of making music, and the changing ways its presentation exploded during the amazing last half of the 20th century—much of what Hancock writes about in *Possibilities* will go right over their heads.

Still, there is much to learn from this book.

The World

Travels with Epicurus: A Journey to a Greek Island in Search of a Fulfilled Life

By Daniel Klein

Reviewed by Fred Beauford

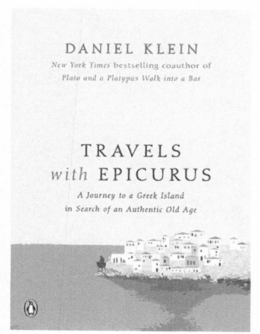

DANIEL KLEIN

New York Times bestselling coauthor of
Plato and a Platypus Walk into a Bar

TRAVELS
with EPICURUS

A Journey to a Greek Island
in Search of an Authentic Old Age

No Zorba

At first, I didn't know quite what to make of this slim volume. Daniel

Klein, an author with many books to his credit, was in his seventies when

his dentist told him he needed tooth implants. But instead of summiting to

at least a year under the drill, he heads to Greece, with a bag of books, to

see if one of his favorite philosophers, Epicurus, could teach him something

about being an old man, with all its many problems, and dreaded fears.

I could tell from the very beginning of this book that this was no robust *Zorba the Greek*. Instead, the author mainly sits alone in Dimitri's Taverna in the village of Kamini on the Greek island of Hydra, and watches closely other old men, natives of this small island, as they spend their final days in close, familiar contact with each other.

As he sits, always keeping a close eye on the old men, he ponders not only Epicurus, but also heavy hitters like Camus, Aristotle, Saint Augustine, Sartre, Aeschylus, Longfellow, Kant, Plato, Nat King Cole and a host of others.

It is clear that Klein puts his degree in philosophy from Harvard to good use here; and it is equally clear that at this stage in his life, he favors the writing of Epicurus because Epicurus believed that old age was the pinnacle of life, the best it gets.

Writes Epicurus: "It is not the young man who should be considered fortunate but the old man who has lived well, because the young man in his prime wanders much by chance, vacillating in his beliefs, while the old man has docked in the harbor, having safeguarded his true happiness."

Yet, despite this sage advice, we find the author himself vacillating from this "safe harbor."

As he admits: "The idea of being an old man safe in the harbor buoys me up as I sit under Dimitri's awning, pondering the best way to spend this stage of my life. It is the notion of being free from vacillating beliefs that gets to me."

Indeed.

Should the aging author Klein take seriously—unsaid, but strongly implied—the famous injunction of the Welsh poet Dylan Thomas: "Do not go gentle into that good night"?

Or, should he follow the example right in front of him of men as old as he, contently staring out at the water, or grazing fondly at a passing, voluptuous young woman, or telling each other the stories that each have heard dozens, if not hundreds of times?

Which could give him the answer and comfort he came so far for?

In the end, this reader had no firm idea. Perhaps it would help if I knew a little more about what led Klein here in the first place, and what his life was like in America. In that sense, there is little blood on the floor, which,

whether we like it or not, can give great clarity to big ideas.

Masters of the Word: How Media Shaped History from the Alphabet to the Internet

By William J. Bernstein

Reviewed by Fred Beauford

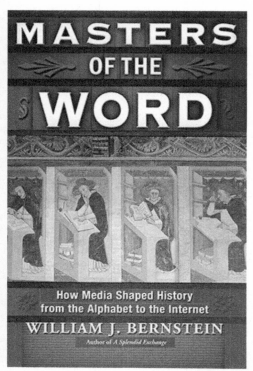

An editor, please

When I first received this book, my immediate reaction was a big thank you to Grove Press for sending it to me. This is a subject I know well, having taught The History of the Mass Media for many years; and although I last taught the subject at Cal State Northridge in 2001, I knew that there was still that little voice that said I might be in the classroom again and maybe this would be a book I could recommend to students.

Three quarters of the way through *Masters of the Word* I recognized that that would be unlikely, not that Bernstein didn't give us a detailed account of the growth of the media, starting with the birth of writing, onward to the development of the internet.

Interwoven with the technical developments, from clay tablets, to papyrus, to paper, to harnessing the conductive power of electricity in the world we now live in, Bernstein also gives us a detailed history lesson on how rulers and elites over the centuries used this new ability to extend and preserve human thought, to oppress and control their subjects; that is, he so aptly points out, until enough people became proficient in whatever became the latest medium, to shake off the people who controlled them.

Bernstein points to the ancient Greeks as an example, who because they developed a large enough literate population, were able to invent democracy, where the concept of ordinary citizens, admittedly literate, had a say in the rules that governed their very existence. (In south of the Sahara Africa at the same time, everyone in the village had a say; they just didn't have a fancy name for it.)

Another example he uses is the impact of the Gutenberg Revolution. Writes Bernstein "…around 1500, we find that industrially produced paper and the printing press amplified the burgeoning literary revolution, and with it, the power of ordinary people to spread their opinions and influence. By the time Martin Luther arrived at the University of Wittenberg its library shelves were already stacked with the fruit of the Gutenberg Revolution. It was not Luther the theologian who affected the Reformation, but rather Luther the publisher."

Bernstein captures well all the key developments of the various media and tries to give us an understanding of how each had a profound impact on humanity. Here is where I have a problem with his book: Bernstein clearly has the scholarship nailed, and I was truly impressed by his vast knowledge. However, he does not have the narrative skills, the chops, if you will, or the ability to self-edit, as a Jared Diamond or Bill Bryson, the two writers his book jacket compares him with.

I grew weary of the endless history lessons that went on and on, when a few paragraphs would have just as easily made the same point. All I could think of is if this guy is putting me the sleep, and this is one of my favorite subjects, I could imagine what this book would do to my students.

It's a shame that what could have been a great book was severely compromised, apparently, by not having a sharp-eyed editor that was more than willing to say enough.

From the Dragon's Mouth: Ten true stories that unveil the real China

By Ana Fuentes

Reviewed by Fred Beauford

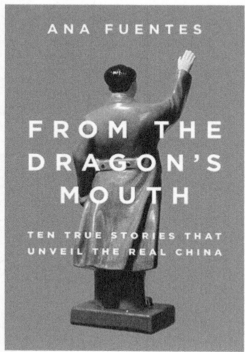

What is Very Chinese?

My friend, Linda Jue, a Chinese-American from the Bay Area, once was describing someone she knew to me: "Well one thing about him, Fred" she observed, "he is *very* Chinese."

I thought I understood what she meant by very, and why she gave it such import. I gave her a small nod.

As an African American I have met more than my share of folks who were very black, and I don't mean in skin color—with an inner self that I could always detect that carried over countless generations, the very soul of Africa.

And, believe it or not, I have also run into some very Americans, small as they may be.

Unlike with many of my fellow countrymen, however, what I didn't know, listening to Linda, was what types of things made someone *very* Chinese.

I, like perhaps most Americans, know little about the largest population on earth. All most of us know, especially wild-eyed greedy capitalists, is a huge, endless army of low paid worker drones and an unbelievably gigantic market for all kinds of goods and services, that had somehow magically materialized out of nowhere.

However, in my mind, it would somehow behoove us to try and understand what my friend Linda meant by her observation, if we are going to understand who we are now locked together with economically.

In the book, From the *Dragon's Mouth*, we get much insight about what makes a Chinese *very* Chinese.

Ana Fuentes, an award-winning journalist from Madrid, Spain, spent four years living and working in China. Fuentes' approach, in her ten chapters, is to look into the lifestyles and attitudes of a broad variety of Chinese citizens in a deeply personal way, mainly, by letting them talk.

This choice, as well as making use of many techniques novelists know well, bore much fruit.

We see, among others, Chinese life through the eyes of the spoiled children of the newly rich; a noted dissenter, imprisoned and tortured by the communist government; a woman married to a homosexual; an aging Kung Fu Master; and she hit pay dirt in terms of Linda's observation, in chapter five, when she profiles Yang Lu.

Here is how she introduces her subject: "This slender, determined woman became a self-made millionaire giving seminars on how to form corporate teams and motivate them.... And speaking about innovation. Only thirty years ago, before the Chinese economy opened up, this would have been unthinkable."

Later, at Yang Lu's large, tasteful suite of offices, "located in a skyscraper in the CBD, one of Beijing's business districts, "the successful entrepreneur outlines her approach to Fuentes, which, in many ways, also gets to the heart of what it means to be Chinese.

" She told me candidly," Fuentes writes, "that the biggest burden holding back Chinese ... was the legacy of Confucius, which dictates a very rigid hierarchical structure. To Confucius, the interest of the group comes before the interests of the individual and maintaining cohesion and harmony had to be the top priority before anything else.

"Yang Lu believed the typical pyramid corporate structure where the bosses give orders and the employees obey fails in the end. In her opinion, the weak point of China's private companies was their lack of experience. The oldest businesses had been in existence for less than three decades (until 1988, they didn't even legally exist) and they had to learn so many things in a hurry."

Fuentes points out that "Today fifty million companies are registered in China, and of those 93% are private. However, the State still controls strategic sectors of the economy through their massive petroleum, gas, cement, insurance and telecommunication firms. Eight of every ten members of the board of directors of these companies are appointed directly by the Communist Party. They are less efficient than private companies, but the major banks, also state-owned, extend the most favorable credit terms to them. Many experts wryly observe that, at the end of the day, they are all part of the same big enterprise: China, Inc."

***

There is much more to be gleamed from this insightful book, and I heartily recommend it. We might as well get to know our new best friend, and *From the Dragon's Mouth* could certainly help in that regard.

Pakistan on the Brink: The Future of America, Pakistan, and Afghanistan
By Ahmed Rashid
Reviewed by Fred Beau ford

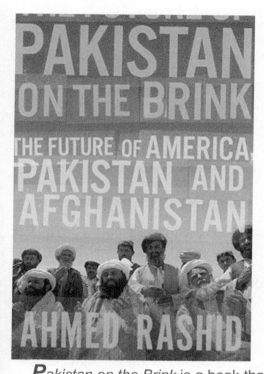

Pakistan on the Brink is a book that bills itself as being about the future fate of two countries, Afghanistan and Pakistan. However, when all is said and done, it is really an interesting, and sometimes scary account of some of the inner workings of present-day Pakistan.

Ahmed Rashid, a Pakistani journalist based in Lapore, presents "a litany of problems" facing Pakistan—most notably, the failure since the partition with India in 1947, to establish a "coherent national identity. Is it not a democracy as envisioned by its founder Muhammad Ali Jinnah? Are its people Muslim first, Hindis or Punjabis second, and Pakistanis third? Or are they Pakistanis first and foremost?" Rashid asks, without giving us an answer, and leaving us to wonder that maybe they are all of the above.

That, for me, more than anything, is a good reason for Rashid to focus his main attention on that troubled country. The Pakistan that the world has come to know, and now fears deeply, was discovered to be a hodge-podge of competing tribes, poverty, corruption, violent Islamic militants, clueless leaders, and a country with" close to one hundred nuclear weapons."

Yet, as Rashid points out, this did not have to be.

..." Pakistan's location gives it enormous geostrategic potential. It borders Central, South, and West Asia, is a gateway to the sea for China, and is situated at the mouth of the Arabian Gulf; no other country in the world has such potential to become a hub for trade and business or the transcontinental transport of energy."

***

So, the question is, why has Pakistan spiraled into disarray, while its neighbors, China and India, have emerged as world leaders in economic growth, and major innovators in many important fields including technology and science?

Rashid places much of the blame on the powerful military: "The military defines Pakistan national identity defensively, in terms of the country's vulnerability, as a national security state, with a permanent mistrust of India. The politicians in power have never seriously tried to challenge this isolating self-definition by offering alternative policies, such as promoting good neighborliness, ending support for Islamic extremism, fostering economic development, and providing education."

He also points a finger at the West, and in particular, the United States, for not fully engaging with both Pakistan and Afghanistan. There is, however, little doubt in his mind that Pakistan is a major problem facing the world.

"The core issue is what happens in Pakistan. Its geostrategic location, its nuclear weapons, its large population, its terrorist camps, and enfeebled economy and polity make it more important—and more vulnerable—than even Afghanistan. And yet Pakistan's plans for its national security consist almost entirely of resisting Indian hegemony, protecting and developing its nuclear program, promoting the Kashmiri cause, and ensuring the presence of a pro-Pakistan government in Kabul."

***

Rashid's insights into the thinking in this part of the world are valuable. One thing I finding missing in this book is a hard look at Islam itself. For example, is a caliphate necessarily a bad idea? Catholics have the Pope. Maybe Muslims need their own kind of living, spiritual leader.

At least there would be a return address for every bomb that went off. These days, it seems that all over the Muslim world, from South of Sahara Africa, North Africa, The Middle East and South Asia, we see bombings, bombings and more bombings, on a daily basis.

Young men seem to be eager to strap on a suicide vest and try to kill as many men, women and children as they can, more often than not, fellow Muslims.

The figures in *Pakistan on the Brink* say that since the war on terror began in 2001, over 225,000 people have been killed in the wars in Afghanistan, Iraq, and Pakistan. But what would the numbers be if we factored in those 40 people killed daily in Africa, and the 30 to 50 killed elsewhere, all in the name of Islam?

These are some hard questions. Maybe author Rashid will address them in his next book.

If he dares.

Historical Heartthrobs: 50 Timeless Crushes—from Cleopatra to Camus

By Kelly Murphy with Hallie Fryd
The Blue Hour
By Patti Davis
Reviewed by Fred Beauford

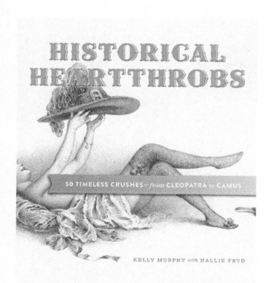

What is Young Adult Literature?

I have been curious about this category of literature for some time. We all know about the enormous success of the Harry Potter series, which made JK Rowling the second richest woman in the United Kingdom.

Also, perhaps with a bit of envy on my part, I think of Walter Myers, who was with me in a writer's workshop at Columbia University, and has gone on to great recognition as a young adult author.

The best-selling book at Morton Books, Inc, was the *Paperboy* pre-teen series. We sold over 50,000 copies and are still selling the four-book series.

But *Paperboy* was not a young adult book; this was a pre-teen book, written by a pre-teen. So what then is young adult literature?

The best explanation I found on the internet was offered by Kay E. Vandergrift of Rutgers, the State University of New Jersey:

"Young adult literature is often thought of as a great abyss between the wonderfully exciting and engaging materials for children and those for adults—just as young adults are often ignored in planning library facilities and services. There is, however, a wealth of fiction created especially for teens that deal with the possibilities and problems of contemporary life as experienced by this age group. These contemporary problem novels reflect the troubled times in which young readers are coming of age, but young people also need to laugh at themselves and at their world and to escape that world in flights of fancy."

***

Historical Heartthrobs: 50 Timeless Crushes—from Cleopatra to Camus, is not fiction. Instead, it profiles 50 historic persons, mixed with a few unknowns. From the provocative cover, with a nearly nude woman lending it great dash, the book promises something that young adults, especially the males, have on their horny little minds all the time: sex.

As I read the book, some of the people author Kelly Murphy writes about did indeed have vigorous sex lives. Including a wily Cleopatra; and Lord Byron, who was said to be so handsome that women fainted when he walked into a room.

And who knew that a gloomy Gus such as Albert Camus, was such a lady's man?

But what are we to make of including such a sexual skinflint as Gloria Steinem, while leaving out the two biggest womanizers of the 20th Century, JFK and Bill Clinton?

Also, for the majority of her subjects, their sex lives were pedestrian, if not non-existent.

The things that writer Murphy did have going for her in *Historical Heartthrob* is her inclusions of a wide variety of people, and her writer's voice, which sounds a lot like the people she is writing to.

In the end, however, this book does not live up to its billing. There were few real "hotties," "peccadilloes," and "noteworthy liaisons," and much of what she writes about her subjects' sex lives is ho-hum heaven.

But, *Historical Heartthrobs: 50 Timeless Crushes* is classic bait and switch. There is some important information contained in this book, and some nice little history lessons, and an interesting way to try and teach history to young adults.

I get it completely.

***

Patti Davis' book *The Blue Hour* is indeed a work of fiction, and it differs from Murphy's book in not only the genre. There is no sex here. Nor is the language young adultish (if there is such a word). Davis clearly has a way with words, and she tells her young readers that they are just going to have to master it.

Davis puts this talent to great use in her novel. It is a ghost story, fulfilling Professor Kay E. Vandergrift words that "young people also need to laugh at themselves and at their world and to escape that world in flights of fancy."

The Blue Hour is quite a fight of fancy, indeed. This is a classic ghost story: a kid comes to a small town and moves into a house where much mysterious trauma had occurred. No mistake about it, we had heard this one before.

But Davis adds something else, which is really the heart of her book: the loner, the daydreamer, the misfit. The kids who are her heroes and heroines, all at some point suffered from acute loneliness and misunderstanding, something many young adults can readily identify with

Davis also has going for *The Blue Hour* her great gift as a storyteller. She moves things around with such a natural gift; and just zips them along. And this is something that all of us editors and publishers love more than anything else, besides money.

With Patti, you just keep turning the pages.

It's What I Do: A Photographer's Life of Love and War
By Lynsey Addario
Reviewed by Fred Beauford

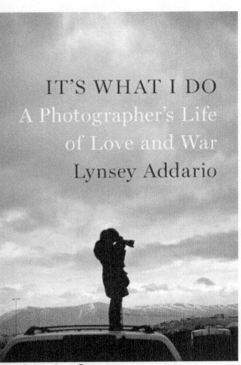

An Amazing Story

When I was in my middle twenties, the same age as Lynsey Addario when she started her amazing journey as a conflict photojournalist, I was doing somewhat of the same thing.

I say "somewhat" deliberately.

I was covering the Long Hot Summer race riots and the growing anti-war demonstrations in late '60s America. Though sometimes harrowing, what I was doing was a mere cakewalk compared to Addario's post 9/11 years of covering conflicts in Afghanistan, Iraq, Lebanon, Darfur and the Congo.

She has dodged bullets, bombs, near starvation and dehydration, and was kidnapped twice, both times feeling that she was surely going to die. All the time she was trying to juggle some semblance of a love life as affair after affair ended because her work got in the way, until she finally found a kindred soul.

What I found most interesting in Addario's book was not the very real drama of covering horrific violence. I might be a jaded reader, but I had already read much of that.

It was her deeply personal insights into the worlds that she covered that most intrigued me.

Here is one insight from the time she was trying to enter Afghanistan during the time of the Taliban rule. She had to apply for a visa to enter the country from Pakistan, and she was given this advice from a fellow journalist before she visited the embassy of the Islamic Emirate of Afghanistan: "Do not look any Afghan man directly in the eye. Keep your head, your face, and your body covered. Don't laugh, or joke under any circumstance. And most important, sit each day in the visa office and drink tea with the visa clerk, Mohammed, to ensure that your application will actually get sent to Kabul and processed."

Later, after she was convinced that she would finally receive her visa, she has one last chat with Mohammed:

Mohammed suddenly leaned forward, glancing through the window to the inside of the main embassy, looking for anyone who might have been listening. There was no one.

"Can I ask you a question?" he whispered.

"Sure, ask me anything, sir," I said, "as long as my answers do not inhibit my getting a visa."

He smiled nervously. "Is it true…," he started. "I mean…I hear that men and women in America go out in public together without being married." He paused again, leaning in to look out the window until he was reassured no one was listening. "That men and women can live together without being married?"

I knew he was taking a chance with the question. The Taliban insists its members renounce sexual curiosity; his anxiety flooded the room.

"Are you sure my answers will not affect whether I get my visa?" I asked.

"I promise you they will not."

"Unmarried men and woman in America spend a lot of time together," I said. "They go on something called 'dates' to movies, to the theater, to restaurants. Men and women sometimes even live together before they marry, and" – unlike in Afghanistan, where most marriages were arranged by and among relatives— "Americans marry for love."

Why was I saying this to a Taliban at the Afghan Embassy? Given the cultural and language barriers between us, I felt certain that he understood no more than 10 percent of what I was saying. But he was enthralled.

"Do men and women…Is it true that men and women touch? And have children before they are married?"

"Yes," I replied gently. "Men and women touch before they are married."

""You are married, right?" He asked.

I smiled, finally comfortable enough to tell him the truth. I don't know why I felt comfortable enough to tell him anything. Maybe because he felt comfortable enough to ask such racy questions? To admit that his mind went to a place forbidden to an unmarried man by the Taliban's severe interpretation of the Koran? "No, Mohammed. I am not married. I lived with a man for a long time—like we were married."

He interrupted me. "What happened? Why did you leave? Why are you not married?"

Mohammed was no longer a Taliban to me. We were simply two people in our twenties, getting to know each other.

"In America women work," I said. "And right now, I am traveling and working."

He smiled. "America is a good place,' he said.

"It is."

Five days later I picked up my visa.

***

This tiny scene, captured brilliantly, better than anything Hollywood could write, and set in a dusty, run down office in Peshawar, Pakistani, spoke clearer to me than all the many books and articles I have read about the great gulf between the West and some of the Islamic world.

***

It was the novelist, not the photographer at work.

***

While Addario's photos are first rate, and scattered throughout the book, it was also evident in *It's What I Do* that she has an uncanny ability to communicate with her subjects, to meet them on a deeply personal level, despite whatever language and cultural barriers she may face, be it with tough Kurd fighters in the north during the invasion of Iraq, or African women dealing with unspeakable violence committed against them in Darfur or the Congo; or even charming some of the dastardly, women hating Taliban, who ruled Afghanistan before they were overthrown by the Americans after 9/11.

Interestingly, it was the American servicemen that gave her much grief as she tried to do the job she was paid to do, sometimes only smirking at her for being "a girl," and sometimes calling her "fucking bitch." She also makes it clear in the book that she did not like President Bush's invasion of Iraq.

Still, her ability to relate to her subjects, seems to me, is part of the reason for the success of her award-winning photography—not just her considerable bravery and technical skills under the direst of circumstances.

This is a must-read book. It is easy to see why Lynsey Addario won a MacArthur Foundation Genius Grant and the Pulitzer Prize for International Reporting.

Shadows of the Pomegranate Tree
By Tariq Ali
Verso 272 pages

Reviewed by Fred Beauford

Tariq Ali

That's Not Islam!

A few years ago, I lived for over two years in a rooming house in Jersey

City, as I ruthlessly crawled my way to literary fame. The person in the

room next to me was a devout Muslim from Pakistan.

He was a handsome young man, beaming with health and well-being,

and with an impressive head of rich looking black hair; that often made me

reluctant to take off my hat in his presence. No point in embarrassing

myself.

His father, I was to soon learn, was a high ranking general in the

Pakistan army; and that bold confidence on my new young friend's

handsome face was always reminding me of that.

One day, as we stood in the shared kitchen, me cooking pork chops, of

which he but would never take a bite, but seemed to enjoy smelling, I got up the courage to ask him what he thought of all the fuss going on in the Mideast and the attack on America on 9/11.

"That's not Islam!" he asserted.

***

In many ways, I found this novel, the first of the *The Islam Quintet,* highly interesting, mainly because of remembering the strong reaction of my young friend from Pakistan. For those who know little about Islam, what we hear often is "That's not Islam." Even our President says that what is happening in the Middle East is not Islam.

***

It turns out that this has been a long, centuries-old struggle to define just what is Islam, if we are to believe *Shadows of the Pomegranate Tree.*

This novel, a reissue for Verso, was first issued by them in 1993.

There are some novelistic conventions I found distracting, and it is mostly all talk, and strange names, with different names for the same person, much like in a classic Russian novel. Still, I found it hard to put down, and couldn't wait to get back to it when I awoke. And I read every page.

Part of the reason was because we see an entire, proud society now forced to choose between religious conversion, exile or the sword.

***

Here is the real bare bones history behind *Shadows of the Pomegranate Tree*, courtesy of Wikipedia:

The Spanish occupation by the Moors began in 711 AD when an African army, under Tariq ibn-Ziyad, crossed the Strait of Gibraltar from northern Africa and invaded the Iberian Peninsula.

The Moors ruled Spain for 800 years. The Moors called the territory Al-Andalus, which at its peak included what is today most of Spain and Portugal. The differences in religions and cultures led to a centuries-long conflict with the Christian kingdoms of Europe, as they tried to reclaim control of Muslim areas,

The Moors were initially of Arab and Berber descent at the time of the Umayyad conquest of Hispania in the early 8th century. Later the term covered people of mixed ancestry (including black Africans), and Iberian Christian converts to Islam (the Arabs called the latter Muwalladun or Muladi)

***

As the novel begins, we are now near the end of what Christian Spain called The Reconquista. Under the leadership of Queen Isabella and King Ferdinand, Muslim and Jewish subjects were offered conversion, exile, or death.

The last Muslim Sultan had fled to North Africa, a place where neither he, nor members of the prominent, prosperous, upper class family at the center of this novel, could only imagine.

Spain was their home. They knew little else. What should they do?

At the heart of this novel, author Tariq Ali, gives us a long, philosophic conversation of what went wrong for the Muslims, after so many years of ruling over *Al-Andalus*. For example, this early passage sets the stage for the rest of the novel in many ways:

The old uncle's mocking voice was still resounding in Umar's head. 'You know the trouble with your religion, Umar. It was too easy for us. The Christians had to insert themselves into the pores of the Roman Empire. It forced them to work below the ground. The catacombs of Rome were their training-ground. When they finally won, they had already built a great deal of social solidarity with their people. Us? The Prophet, peace be upon him, sent Khalid bin Walid with a sword and he conquered. Oh yes, he conquered a great deal. We destroyed two empires. Everything fell into our lap. We kept the Arab lands and Persia and parts of Byzantium. Elsewhere it was difficult, wasn't it? Look at us. We have been in Al-Andalus for seven hundred years and still we could not build something that would last. It's not just the Christians, is it, Umar? The fault is in ourselves.'

Near the end of the novel, another character echo's this: "Our own fault," declared Ibn Hisham without a shadow of a doubt. "We always look for answers in the actions of our enemies…Our Prophet died too soon, before he could consolidate the new order. His successors killed each other like the warring tribesmen that they were. Instead of assimilating the stable characteristics of civilizations which we conquered, we decided instead on imparting to them our own mercurial style."

Shades of Pat Roberson!

The novel goes on like this, always pointing to the bickering among Muslims about just what Prophet Mohammed really said, and how should it be interpreted. This first book was published in 1991. All hell had not yet broken out in the Middle East between Muslims. This is a thoughtful book that explains much of what we witness almost every time we turn on the news.

Evolving Ourselves: How Unnatural Selection and Nonrandom Mutations are Changing Life on Earth

By Juan Enriquez and Steve Gullans

Portfolio/Penguin | 2015 | 352 pages

Reviewed by Fred Beauford

Juan Enriquez

Photo Credit:
John Werner

Will the choice then be a better God, or no God?

I am sometimes amazed at the direction reading books can take my mind. As I read this highly interesting science book, all I could think of was theology and especially monotheism.

I should add, in fairness to *Evolving Ourselves*, that the authors in no way deal with religion, although, in many ways, the book is all about religion—it is only a quirk in my own mind that that led to this essay.

In monotheism, this all-knowing, all-seeing, personal god revealed itself some 5,000 years ago in the burning deserts of the Mideast.

Our two authors point out that "About 7,500 generations ago, our type, *Homo sapiens,* began to build, create, and pillage small villages. What we refer to as "civilization" began about 500 generations ago, with the advent of agriculture."

In other words, when this god was first conceived we were a wild "all natural" species, surrounded by other "all natural" species, who wanted nothing more than to have us for lunch.   That was before we started creating unnatural environments.

"Unnatural environments have been very good for humans" the authors of *Evolving Ourselves* points out, "as we domesticated ourselves and our environments, we gradually removed the obstacles to a long life span. For most of our history, for most people, days were filled with malnutrition, disease, and violence. A major concern was to not get eaten. Predators of all kinds were far more common until our massive and deliberate kill-off modified our environment to such an extent that we must search really carefully to find any of the most-common big animal predators."

Steve Gullans
PhotoCredit:
Jeff Thiebauth

But you can also see why we craved something, or someone to look over us, protect us, to allow us to live. So what if we had to bow down to it daily! That was a small price to pay.

All kinds of gods sprang up, but the one that finally captured much of the world was the demanding god of the Hebrews. And now, that god, who now has many names, is wedded to the amazing technical progress *Homo sapien* has made, which is well documented in *Evolving Ourselves*.

Now, we have become the architect, the creative designer, and have managed to sanitize much of our lives, and *Evolving Ourselves* points out that even more wonders are coming. And, I might add, much dread that we just might be too smart for our own good.

So, do we still need this god of the desert? Does it boil down to continuing to worship an ancient, irrelevant god? Or, no god at all, as Friedrich Nietzsche would have it?

Daily, headlines tell us that the desert people that created monotheism, and refined it over the years, seem to think we need this god, now more than ever; and many of them are willing to destroy the entire world in the name of their god.

But the question for me is that if we can create this brilliant new world the authors of *Evolving Ourselves* give us, still beset with dangers, to be sure, but far better than anything before it, all by using this wonderful mind we are blessed with—can we now create a better, more peaceful god?

Vacation Guide to the Solar System
By Olivia Koski and Jana Grcevich
Reviewed by Fred Beauford

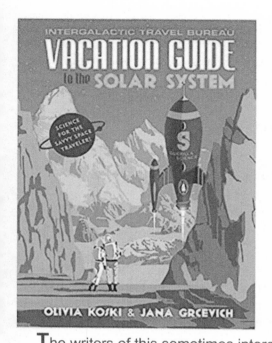

The writers of this sometimes interesting book set the stage exactly right in the very first paragraph. "Some may question the wisdom of creating a vacation guide to the planets," Koski and Grcevich write, "when human feet haven't touched the ground of another world (the moon) since 1972. If you're thinking that a space vacation is a distant fantasy, however, remember that one hundred years ago, airplanes were a cutting-edge technology. The fast ones could travel at the "great speed" of 120 miles an hour, bringing a prospective space traveler to Neptune in 2,571 years. In 1989, the Voyager 2 spacecraft reached Neptune in less than twelve years traveling at 42,000 miles per hour. One hundred years from now, who knows how long a trip to Neptune might take?

"Assuming we don't destroy ourselves first, humans will go to places we describe in this book someday, almost without question."

The authors then take us on a journey to all the planets in the solar system and point out in the three rocky planets, Mercury, Venus and Mars, where we have already sent probes to map the terrain—all of the natural features for the vacationer. To be frank, I found little on these planets of interest. Just a lot of bad weather. My great interest in Mars, besides perhaps viewing Mount Olympus, the tallest extinct volcano in the solar system, is, did life on Earth begin on Mars? We now know with certainty that Mars once had an atmosphere and vast oceans of water, but did it also have life? And did chunks of Mars, break of and find its way to our oceans? It certainly did in my novella, *A History of the 21st Century.*

It is when we get to the gas giants, with the granddaddy of them all, Jupiter, that I became excited to see what more I could learn about them. When you get to Jupiter that is when our "vacation" really began, not only because this planet "is a planet of storms, force of nature, with a mass far greater than that of the rest of the planets in the solar system combined. His power is intoxicating."

But, it is not just Jupiter itself. Our two authors write, "Though it's easy to become hypnotized by the planet's sand sculpture cloudbursts, it's the moons that will seduce you. The Jovian system is a solar system within a solar system, hosting satellites as varied as—some even bigger than—planets."

We have learned much since that groundbreaking PBS series, *Cosmos: A Personal Voyage,* first was aired by a PBS affiliate, KCET in 1978 and was presented by Carl Sagan. Now, the Science Channel can give anyone who cares to listen in, updated information about wormholes, quantum mechanics, death stars, merging galaxies, multiple and parallel universes, where there might be millions of me walking around, string theory, and on and on, including a close look at our own tiny solar system, which has turned out to be more interesting than we could ever imagined just a few decades before, including a close looks at the moons of Jupiter, all 67 of them, including the most interesting ones like Io, Europa, Ganymede; and also, Saturn's mighty moon, Titan, and all the other moons of the gas giant.

As I have said, *Vacation Guide to the Solar System* is sometimes very interesting, but I will also say, try the Science Channel. It will give you goosebumps discovering all the things that can come out of nowhere from our vast universe and ruin your day.

Made in the USA
Coppell, TX
04 September 2020